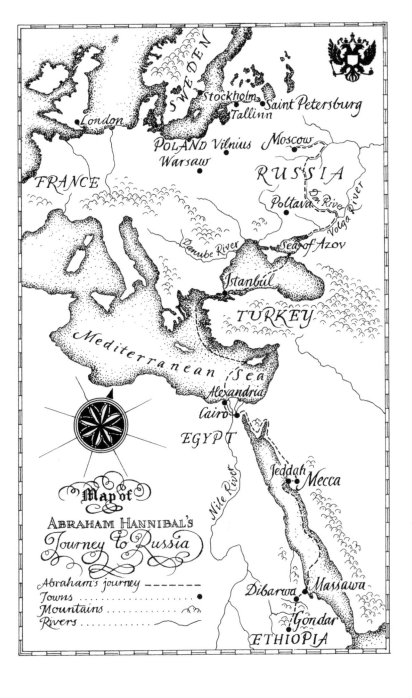

London

SWEDEN
Stockholm
Tallinn
Saint Petersburg

POLAND Vilnius
Warsaw

Moscow

RUSSIA

FRANCE

Poltava
Don River
Volga River

Danube River
Sea of Azov

Istanbul

TURKEY

Mediterranean Sea

Alexandria

Cairo

EGYPT

Nile River

Jeddah Mecca

Map of

ABRAHAM HANNIBAL'S
Journey to Russia

Abraham's journey --------
Towns .... •
Mountains .... ᨈ
Rivers ....

Dibarwa Massawa

Gondar

ETHIOPIA

Also by Frances Somers Cocks
Abraham Hannibal and
the Raiders of the Sands

For Nina
with love from

ABRAHAM
HANNIBAL

and the Battle for the Throne

Frances Somers Cocks

FRANCES SOMERS COCKS

ILLUSTRATED BY ERIC ROBSON

GOLDHAWK · PRESS

First published in Great Britain in 2003 by
the Goldhawk Press
19 Kempson Road, London SW6 4PX
email goldhawkpress@btopenworld.com

Produced for the Goldhawk Press by
Umberto Allemandi e C., Turin – London - Venice

Printed and bound in Italy

ISBN 0 9544034 1 X

British Library Cataloguing-in-Publication Data: a catalogue record
for this book is available from the British Library

*The front cover illustration, by Eric Robson, shows Abraham in front of St Basil's Cathedral
in Red Square, Moscow*

for Abraham Alexander
- his book

WHAT THEY SAID ABOUT THE ABRAHAM HANNIBAL BOOKS …

"A lively, startlingly original adventure story with a most satisfying basis in historical fact. Frances Somers Cocks is full of surprises and has a wonderfully strong empathy with the child at the centre of the story." **Libby Purves**

"I loved the look of it – those illustrations are great." **Benjamin Zephaniah**

"A brilliant idea – she has turned the story of Pushkin's Ethiopian ancestor into a thrilling, original and deeply exotic adventure. I wish I'd been able to read it when I was ten – but it's lovely now." **Ruth Padel**

"This is a wonderful tale, full of exciting adventure, and with a wealth of colourful detail. Frances Somers Cocks achieves the rare feat of taking young readers by the hand and leading them surefootedly to another time and place." **Will Self**

ABOUT THE AUTHOR

Frances Somers Cocks has been a teacher in England, Africa, Spain and China. This has been handy, because she has been able to use the school holidays to go travelling in Abraham Hannibal's footsteps and to research and write his story. Her journeys have been by bus, lorry, camel, train and boat, and have mostly been uncomfortable but good fun. She has never been shipwrecked or captured by pirates, though she did get into terrible trouble with her head-teacher once, when her boat got stuck in the Red Sea and she got back to school two weeks late (not that the children were bothered!)

Frances Somers Cocks lives in London with her son Abraham Alexander and a ginger tom-cat called Nimrod, in a messy flat full of weird and lovely pictures, carvings and ornaments from all over the world – but especially from the countries where Abraham Hannibal lived.

CONTENTS

GLOSSARY AND GUIDE TO PRONUNCIATION

ambassador a special messenger from a King
   or government to a foreign country
Barbary Coast the old name for th coast of North Africa
cavalry the part of an army that fights on horseback
Charles XII (say Charles the Twelfth) the King of Sweden
   at the time of this story
colony country ruled by a foreign country
Doctor Poncet (say PON-say) a French doctor
   to the Ethiopian Emperor
Fares (say FAR-res) Abraham's father, a Prince known
   as the Lord of the Sea
Frank a white person, a person from northern Europe;
   a French person
galley a small, fast ship with oars or sail
galley-slave a slave forced to row a galley
gunner a soldier in charge of a cannon
Hannibal a famous African General who attacked
   the Ancient Roman Empire
hold the lower part of a ship, used for carrying cargo
Holy of Holies the most important, secret part
   of an Ethiopian or Russian church
infantry the part of an army that fights on foot
Lahia (say La-HEE-a) Abraham's older sister,
   his only full sister

lily-flower the symbol of France

Louis XIV (say Lou-ee the Fourteenth) the King of France at the time of this story; also known as the Sun King

mare a female horse

mosque Muslim holy house of prayer

musket an old-fashioned type of gun

regiment a large section of an army

page-boy a boy working for an important person, such as a lord or King

port the left-hand side of a ship

starboard the right-hand side of a ship

Sultan the all-powerful ruler of the vast Turkish Empire

Tsar the King of Russia

Chapter 1

CAPTURED AGAIN!

"RUN!" the boy screamed. "RUN FOR YOUR LIFE!"

He turned and started running back up the beach towards the hillside, but it was too late. For the second time in his life, he felt himself grabbed, turned upside down, and carried off over a man's shoulder.

There was a loud noise of laughing and talking, and then a terrible thump and a hot, scraping pain in his hands and face and knees as he was thrown violently, face down, into the bottom of a little boat; then the girl was dumped down there too. He felt his wrists yanked roughly behind his back and tied, his legs tied at the knees, and then the boat was tugged along the water's edge, crunching on the pebbly bottom.

At last the men seemed to reach the place they wanted, and Abraham felt the little boat rocking wildly as they lifted out great water-barrels. Out of the corner of his eye, he could see them heave the barrels over the sides, and he and the girl were left alone in the bottom of the boat.

"Are you ... are you ... all right ... Nagonga?" groaned Abraham.

"I think yes ... but who are these men? I'm sure ... I heard them talking ... Arabic."

"Yes, I heard them too, though it's not much like the kind of Arabic I know ... They're pirates - they must be. That French ship out there can't be ... it can't be theirs ... they must have captured it."

Abraham was still lying with his face against the salty, soaking bottom of the boat.

"What are they doing now? I can't see a thing."

With a lot of wriggling and grunting, he managed to turn himself round so that he was facing upwards. Nagonga was on the other side of the boat, her hands and legs tied too, but at least she was already on her back. She had even managed to half-sit up. But all the two children could see was the wooden planks of the boat's sides.

Abraham closed his eyes. His bruised knees throbbed, and the scraped skin on his face and hands and legs stung, but far worse than that was the cold, sick feeling of complete despair.

I'm back where I started. I'm a slave again. I never got free at all.

Suddenly, he felt a gentle kick against his leg.

"Abraham? Are you all right?"

Somehow, Nagonga had wriggled over so that she could just touch him with her foot.

"Listen, Abraham, maybe it is not so bad. We are alive, and at least this way we are leaving the island. Somehow, we will escape, won't we? We'll find a way to escape. We *can* escape, if we really want to."

He smiled at Nagonga, and nodded. She really *was* just like his sister – that was exactly what Lahia would have said.

If you want something badly enough, and don't give up wanting it, you'll get it in the end. That's what

Lahia always said. She wouldn't want me to give up hope.

Very firmly, Abraham said, "You're right, Nagonga. We'll escape."

Just then, the men started coming back to the boat. They were fierce-faced and bearded, wearing wide sailors' trousers and bright short jackets and white turbans wound round red caps; each one had a shining curved dagger at his waist. They threw four goats bleeding from great knife-gashes across their throats, and with their feet tied, down into the boat, and then four live goats, their feet tied together too. Then they started bringing the water-barrels back, heaving them into the boat with a lot of cursing and tipping and splashing.

"One of these water-things can kill us if they throw it on us by a mistake," exclaimed Nagonga.

"I know," said Abraham, who had already wriggled as far out of the way as he could, so that he was almost on top of the heap of dead and live goats. "Move back a bit!"

At last the pirates rowed the little boat back to the big ship, and a rope ladder was thrown down. They climbed up nimbly, lifting the goats up by their tied feet.

Then Nagonga gave a great scream, as a pirate picked her up, flung her over his shoulder, and quickly swung himself up the ladder and dropped her onto the deck of the big ship. Abraham braced himself, and found himself hauled up too, his bare feet scraping against the roughness of the ladder, and then dumped down on deck next to Nagonga. A crowd of other sailors gathered round to stare down at them, laughing and exclaiming.

Soon Abraham felt himself picked up again and carried along the deck, and then down a ladder into a dark and stinking cargo-hold, where Nagonga was quickly dumped down next to him, and the ropes round their wrists and legs were cut.

Chapter 2

THE CARGO OF FRANKS

The children sat for a while, aching and dizzy, unable to see where they were, until at last their eyes got used to the gloom. They were in a big cargo-hold, full of barrels and bundles and boxes, a few port-holes near the top giving a little light.

At one side was an area clear of cargo, with makeshift beds on the floor, a few plates and mugs and buckets - and the biggest number of white people that they had ever seen in their lives, at least twenty or thirty of them, lying or sitting on the floor, silently staring at them. All of them were men, except for one boy of about ten and a girl of sixteen or so.

Abraham had seen pictures of white people (Franks, he called them); he had even known a few himself – but they hadn't looked anything like this.

Where are their fine white wigs and their shining clothes? They're just wearing rags! They look so dirty and weak and exhausted …

Nagonga was looking at them in bewilderment.

"Are *these* Franks, Abraham? They are … they are not how I expected them to look from your stories!"

"No, but I'm sure this is their ship, and the pirates have stolen it from them."

Abraham got up and, hobbling stiffly at first, his shoulders and knees and wrists stabbing with pain, came nearer to the group of Franks. He wanted to do a fine French-style bow, but it didn't seem quite right down here in this gloomy, stinking cargo-hold.

He cleared his throat, licked his dry lips, and began one of the French sentences he'd learnt, long ago in Ethiopia.

"My name is Abraham, and my father is a noble lord of Africa ..."

A few of the Franks sat up and looked at him, and muttered at each other. One man, a solid, kind-faced man who was sitting with the two white children, one arm around each of them, looked suddenly alert, and rattled off a lot of words that Abraham couldn't make head nor tail of. He seemed to finish with a question.

There was a silence. Abraham didn't know what to say, so he said another of his French sentences.

"The Emperor of Ethiopia sends brotherly greetings to the King of the Franks."

Some of the Franks smiled, and the man with the children asked him something else. Abraham replied with almost the last of his stock of French sentences,

"France is a most beautiful and interesting country. I have a lion called Nimrod. My mother is called Makeda and my father is called Fares. My sister is called Lahia ..."

He broke off.

No, my sister WAS called Lahia ... I don't even know how to say that in French ... I really feel a fool, repeating all these stupid foreign sentences I've learnt off by heart ...

The man with the children jabbered at him some more, and paused. Then he suddenly switched to something that Abraham understood:

"I think I heard you speaking Arabic with your … your sister, is she? Can you speak Arabic?"

"Peace be with you!" replied Abraham at once, in Arabic.

"And peace be with you, Abraham! You seem to be a remarkable boy, even if your French is rather limited."

The barrier was down!

Abraham called back through the darkness at Nagonga,

"Nagonga, come here! The Frank speaks Arabic! We can talk to the Franks!"

Chapter 3

SLAVE STORIES

Soon the ship's whole story came out, as the children sat at the Frank's feet in the dark cargo-hold.

"This is a French ship, *The Star of the Sea*," began the Frank, still sitting with one arm around each of his children. "We were sailing from the port of Marseilles, in the south of France, to Naples, and then to Sicily. We had a cargo of cloth, china and tapestries for Naples, and wheat and New World sugar and tobacco for Sicily. But I was on my way with my children to work as a merchant in Sicily, a merchant in wine. I am an Englishman, and I have worked as a merchant all my life, in many different countries,

The Mediterranean Sea

in England, in France, in Italy and in Egypt. My wife passed away in France, two years ago, and so I am father *and* mother to these two children of mine." And he gave them each a squeeze and a smile.

The Frankish boy and girl clearly couldn't understand what he was saying, but they smiled back up at him. To tell the truth, Abraham and especially Nagonga couldn't quite follow all of the Frank's story, since he kept mentioning strange places and things that they'd never heard of.

"My daughter is called Elizabeth, and my son Andrew. They are Elizabeth and Andrew Robertson, since I am Mr Robertson."

Abraham practised the names under his breath. Even in the gloom of the cargo-hold, he was fascinated by the way the Robertsons looked.

How strange … they've all three of them got blue eyes … and the children's hair is so yellow and so long … it all seems … well … a bit against nature … not ugly, just odd … Hey, they're staring back at me now … I wonder if Nagonga and I look just as strange to them …

The Frank said something very fast to his

children in their language, as if explaining what he'd been saying in Arabic.

"To carry on ... we had unloaded our cargo in Naples, and we were sailing south along the coast towards Sicily, when a huge storm blew up. We were driven right off course, far out to sea, and lost one of our masts and some of our sails. But at last the storm was over, and we found a galley rowing towards us, in a much worse state than we were, in fact looking about ready to sink. We let it come alongside, and the crew boarded us, and it was then that we realised they were

pirates, the terrible pirates of the Barbary Coast of Africa. Our cannons had been no use at all. We tried to fight them off, but our captain and half the crew were killed, and the rest of us found ourselves prisoners in our own cargo-hold."

"But what is going to happen to us all?" asked Abraham.

Mr Robertson's face grew suddenly very serious. "I fear that we are being taken to the big market in Istanbul, to be sold as slaves. The Turks always need more men to row their galleys for them, and they often capture Christians to be their galley-slaves. I suppose, if my son is luckier, he might even be taken into the Sultan's Palace as a page-boy, and rise to great things in the court ... though still as a slave, mind, and he must give up his Christian faith. As for my daughter ... with her golden locks and white skin ... I fear ... I very much fear ... she will be bought as a slave by some great man ...who knows, even by the Sultan of Turkey himself ...."

Mr Robertson pressed his lips hard together, and in the darkness of the cargo-hold, Abraham could see tears shining in the corners of his eyes. He had never seen a grown man weep before.

"But I am hoping it won't come to that. I may be able to get a message to some business friends in France or England or Italy to send money to buy our freedom."

"What about Nagonga and me?"

Mr Robertson shook his head. "House-slaves, most likely. At least it's better than farm-work. They don't treat their house-slaves badly in Turkey, not the way our sugar-colonies and tobacco-colonies do. But how do two Africans happen to be here? What is your story? Why were you speaking in French of the King of the Franks and the ... the Emperor of Ethiopia, was it?"

Abraham started off fast and excitedly.

"Well, you see, the Emperor of Ethiopia – that's our Emperor Jesus the Great – chose me and nine other noble children to go with his doctor, Doctor Poncet, on a mission to France. I am of the line of Solomon, King of the Jews – my father is Fares, the Lord of the Sea, a great man in my country. We were taking gifts and a message of friendship to the Sun King, King Louis of the Franks. That's why Doctor Poncet taught me some French – I've been practising ever since, so I won't forget! My sister, Lahia ... my sister Lahia ... she wanted to come with me, so she tried to swim after our ship ... and she ... she ... drowned ..."

In spite of himself, Abraham's voice began to crack, and he could feel the tears starting to come. Nagonga and Mr Robertson each took one of his hands, and the two Frankish children whispered something to their father; Mr Robertson whispered back to them in their own language, and then said,

Abraham Hannibal

"I was telling my children what you were saying. They are very sad about your loss."

Abraham smiled at them all, and swallowed hard.

"It's … it's all right. Anyway, we got as far as Arabia, but we were kidnapped by the King of Mecca and his desert raiders – Doctor Poncet wasn't, I never found out what happened to him – and I was sold to a Turkish merchant called Master Ahmet."

Abraham shivered for a moment at the thought of that bony, wrinkled face, the cold, scornful look in those eyes, that whining voice forever nagging at him …

"Master Ahmet took me to Egypt and put me and lots of other slaves and goods on a ship … that's where I met Nagonga. Of course, she isn't my sister as you thought – but she's like a sister now. Anyway, there was a huge storm, and the ship was wrecked on this tiny island. We were the only two slaves who survived. We lived on the island for 37 days - I counted. I marked the days on a stick!"

Mr Robertson looked startled, and explained the story to his children. The children fired some questions at him, and he laughed,

"We all want to know what you lived on for so long."

"Goats' milk and cheese – we made it ourselves. Luckily there were lots of goats there - that's why we gave the island the name Goat Island. We built a hut too. And then your ship came, and we thought we were safe! I saw the lily-flower flag, so I knew this was a French ship, with Christian sailors who would never take a Christian as a slave. I was sure it would take us to France, and I would achieve my mission to the Sun King after all, and show him that the youth of Ethiopia are second to none, just as my Emperor asked me to. And now look where we are instead!"

For a terrible moment, as Abraham looked around his gloomy prison, he thought he might break down again, and Nagonga caught his eye and said drily,

"I told you that perhaps we go from the crocodile's teeth into the lion's claws, remember?"

Mr Robertson was grim-faced, looking at the skinny boy in his torn and dirty under-shorts.

Abraham Hannibal

"My boy, even if *The Star of the Sea* were still a Christian ship under a Christian captain, I wouldn't place too much hope in your reaching the French court. I believe every word you've told me, but many wouldn't, and there's many a Christian ship whose daily business is carrying slaves to a living death in the Americas."

Abraham stared at him in disbelief.

"But I am a Christian, just like you Franks! Surely a Frank would never sell another Christian into slavery? Surely not!"

"Well, they'll more commonly sell pagans or Muslims - but most Frankish slave-merchants will happily buy and sell any African they can lay their hands on, Christian or otherwise. Countless so-called Christians have this fearful stain on their souls, I'm sorry to say. Let's hear your tale now, Nagonga. It's your turn."

So Nagonga told the story of her village far, far away in the south, in the Land of the Black People, where the Great River flows through a vast green swamp, and how she and her friends were out collecting firewood when slave-raiders caught them and packed them on little boats and took them down the Great River, on a journey so terrible that two of her friends threw themselves into the water rather than endure it one more day; then at last they reached the sea and Master Ahmet's ship, and her story and Abraham's became the same story, ending in this dark cargo-hold …

At last two pirates came down with water and flat dry bread for them all, and soon the dim light faded from the port-holes, and they all stretched themselves on the hard floor to sleep.

Abraham lay awake for a long time, listening to the steady breathing of the others asleep around him. It was hard getting used to the rocking of a boat again, after 37 days on dry land … and, besides, his mind was racing …

Here we are, then … we did escape to the Franks, just as I hoped we would, and they're no better off than we are … every one of us a slave, and what's the Sun King going to do about it?

But then the thought of his sister Lahia came to him:

If you want something badly enough, and don't

give up wanting it, you'll get it in the end … that's what you always used to say, Lahia, isn't it? … The Sun King isn't going to find me, so I'll just have to find him. I'll get my message to King Louis, I'll show him that the youth of Ethiopia is the best in the world for wisdom and courage and high breeding, just as our Emperor said …

And, under his breath, but very firmly, Abraham repeated, like a magic charm, two of the sentences that the French doctor had taught him in Ethiopia:

"My name is Abraham, and my father is a noble lord of Africa. The Emperor of Ethiopia sends brotherly greetings to the King of the Franks."

Chapter 4

INTO THE UNKNOWN

The next morning, as the dawn light feebly began to shine through the port-holes, *The Star of the Sea* set sail, and made her way out from the little harbour into the open sea. Even Mr Robertson, who was used to calendars and maps, had no idea, as the ship churned through the waves, of where they were or what day it was, though the dawn light shining every morning through the starboard port-holes, and the evening sun glowing from the port side told him that they were going north.

Andrew and Elizabeth had already discovered that if they stood on their father's shoulders they could see out of the port-holes, and the other two children soon copied them, but all they could see was empty sky, and

sometimes the empty sea, if the ship was pitching that way, or at best the smoky grey bulk of distant islands, or perhaps the mainland of Turkey.

Every day's food was more or less the same: water and some flat bread in the morning, piles of some yellow grainy stuff and some gristly, bony goat stew in the middle of the day, and a bit more water and bread in the evening.

Twice they came into shore - to get water, they supposed - but as none of the prisoners were allowed out of the hold, it didn't make much difference. Only the weather changed: days

when the ship swooped onwards fast and smoothly, days when she pitched and lurched in violent gusts of wind, days when it hardly moved at all, and the air down in the cargo-hold grew hot and heavy and stale. But there were no more bad storms.

In between meals and sleeping and peering at the view, Abraham and Nagonga showed the other children how to play their favourite game, on a board scratched out on the floor with charcoal, and sometimes Mr Robertson or even the other Franks had a go, and then Andrew and Elizabeth showed the other children how to play a game called chess, and Mr Robertson kept interfering and helping whoever was losing.

Abraham showed Andrew and Elizabeth and Nagonga how to write their names in his own alphabet, the one that he had learnt when he was still living at home in Ethiopia, marking out the swirling, twisting letters on the floor with

scraps of charcoal, but they refused completely to learn the whole alphabet:

"Two hundred and forty letters! What d'you need so many for? Twenty-six is plenty!"

And Andrew and Elizabeth taught the other two children their alphabet, all twenty-six letters, although Abraham did feel surest only of the letters that came up in their names: Elizabeth, Andrew, Nagonga, Abraham.

When it was too dark for writing or games, there were stories, of course: they all told them, and Mr Robertson was kept busy translating between Arabic and English, or Arabic and French if some of the sailors wanted to take part. And somehow the ship's dark cargo-hold seemed a happier place than before Abraham and Nagonga were thrown down into it at Goat Island.

Chapter 5

THE SLAVE-MARKET

At last the voyage ended, and they saw real daylight again. If Abraham had kept his counting-stick with him, the marks would have shown Day 49 since the shipwreck, and Day 12 since he and Nagonga were captured by the *Star of the Sea.*

They heard the capital of the Sultan's Empire long before they saw it. For hours, as the sea grew narrower and busier, there was the shouting of distant sailors, the creaking of the rigging of other ships passing nearby, the plop of the oars of rowing-boats.

Then, as *The Star of the Sea* moored along some dockside, there was the crashing of cargoes being loaded and unloaded all around them, the braying of donkeys, the yelling of sailors and porters and merchants and officials and street-sellers. But they could hardly see anything through the port-holes that they could make sense of.

At last, half-a-dozen pirates came down into the hold with pistols in their hands, and pushed them up the ladder one by one; they were greeted at the top by more pirates, who immediately tied their hands behind their backs.

It was evening, but still the light made them all blink and squint and try to wipe their eyes. And as at last Abraham started to see clearly, he saw that this was a city like no other, not even Cairo. High above him, past the dock-side, rose great long hills, where vast mansions, and gigantic mosques with round domed roofs ranged from the water's edge up to the very top, seeming to float one above the other, and countless sharp tall towers pierced the sky.

On the other side of a narrow inlet of sea were more hills, more huge buildings and towers, and beyond that a wider reach of water and more land again, far away. And as he looked, a cry rang out from every one of the tall towers,

a cry he knew from Mecca and Cairo and the long days of trudging through the desert:

ALLAH AKBAR! GOD IS GREAT!

The men on the dockside bowed down and said their evening prayers, and so did a few of the pirates, but most didn't bother, and soon Abraham, Nagonga and the Franks were being pushed down the gang-plank and marched along steep and crowded alley-ways up the hillside, until at last they came to a tall, wide

stone building with huge wooden gates. They were led inside into an enormous courtyard.

It was a bit like the merchants' inns and markets that Abraham kept having to go to in Cairo, running errands for Master Ahmet: a courtyard with a little mosque in the middle, and all around it a huge oblong of big open stalls on the ground floor and three more floors above them, with a great long balcony running round each floor, overlooking the courtyard, and lots and lots of little rooms opening off the balconies, all with strong wooden doors.

Istanbul: The Slave-Market

In the merchants' inns in Cairo, the courtyards had been a hubbub of camels and donkeys, and boxes and bundles of goods being loaded or unloaded, and the little rooms had been where the merchants slept and drank tea and stored their goods, but this market was different. Abraham stood, and stared and stared.

There they all were, men, women and children, but especially women and children, tall and short, stocky and slim, their skins every shade, light brown, dark brown, white, deep blue-black; hair blonde and brown and red and black, long and straight, curly, frizzy; dark faces scarred with the scars of deepest Africa, round faces, long faces, thin faces, snub-nosed faces and sharp-nosed faces ...

This was the most famous slave-market of the East: the slave-market of Istanbul. This was the home, for one day, or two, or twenty, until they were sold, of countless humans who would never see their real homes again.

Abraham Hannibal

Elizabeth was the first to go, on the very first morning. The pirates had handed their whole batch of prisoners over to a local slave-merchant who was going to sell them off, and had gone back to their ship.

The slave-merchant took Elizabeth away, and had her dressed up in fine robes of silk and velvet; they saw her as she was led off afterwards to a separate pavilion at the far end of the courtyard where most of the white women and girls seemed to be put up for sale, and then again as she was taken out of the market by a procession of fat old black men in magnificent robes and enormously tall hats.

Mr Robertson was standing with the other Franks and the children in a kind of raised pen. He had one arm round Andrew, the other round Abraham and Nagonga, as if they could somehow stand in for Elizabeth.

He murmured something in Andrew's ear in English, and then said in Arabic, for the other two children, "Those are the Sultan's officials, I'll swear. It's just as I feared. She has gone to the Sultan's Palace, to join his slave-girls."

And Mr Robertson began to shake with

violent, silent sobs, and children hugged him and each other, tighter and tighter, as if somehow they could squeeze the sobs into stopping.

Andrew was bought that afternoon, picked by more Government officials to become one of the Sultan's White Slave-Guards. Two days later, Mr Robertson and most of the Franks from the *Star of the Sea* were bought as galley-slaves.

The same day, a wrinkled old man and his veiled wife came and looked at Nagonga's ears and teeth and finger-nails and, after a lot of arguing over the price, took her to off to be trained as a cook.

Abraham sat in a corner of the sales-pen, feeling completely blank, empty, not even able to cry.

Good-bye. It's always good-bye. Goodbye to every friend I've ever had …

Abraham Hannibal

That night, Abraham sat slumped on the cobbles of the courtyard, near some slave-children talking and laughing round a fire. They were black, like him, and were chatting in broken Arabic. He could have joined in, but it all seemed too much effort. How *could* they laugh in this place?

Suddenly, someone was speaking to him, in a language he couldn't understand. He looked up. A little old white man, a Turk by his clothes, was looking down at him, in quite a kindly way.

"I don't understand you," muttered Abraham grumpily in Arabic.

The old man switched over to Arabic.

"Unhappiness will not help you, child. God has given us a hard life, and we must make the best of it."

"It's all very well for you to say that, but you're free. I'm a slave. I didn't ask to be here."

"No. I am a slave too. I work here, for the Keeper of the Slave-Market."

In spite of himself, Abraham sat up straighter.

"How did *you* come to be a slave?"

Istanbul: The Slave-Market

The old man came and squatted down next to Abraham.

"I was born in a cold land far to the north of here, in a country called Russia. Every year wild horsemen come from the south and raid our villages, carrying off our most beautiful girls, our finest young boys, and bring them to this market for sale. The girls are taken into the Palaces of the greatest lords, or even - if they are very lovely - into the Palace of the Sultan himself, while the boys join the Sultan's army, or become page-boys in his Palace, or galley-slaves in his ships."

The old man shook his head sadly.

"I was not a strong boy, or well-made, but I was taken too, and bought by the Keeper of the Slave-Market to do cleaning here. I have known countless slaves come into this market and go out again, and I know that if they give up hope, they will soon sicken and die."

"But most of the Frankish slaves seem to go on to lead a fine life in Palaces," said Abraham. "What about us black ones? Why do we get all the hard work? What have we got to hope for in that sort of life?"

"Even if you are sweeping the floor of your master's house, you are as much a child of God as he is, and you are worth every bit as much. Tell me, what is your name?"

"Abraham."

"Well, Abraham, did you ever hear the story of Hannibal the African?"

Abraham shook his head.

"Well, long, long ago, far away in North Africa, there lived a boy called Hannibal. His father was king of that land, and for many years he waged war against a mighty empire, the most powerful that the world had ever known: the Empire of Rome. At last his father, the king, was about to die, and still he had not defeated the Roman enemy. And on his death-bed he made the boy Hannibal swear that he would never give in to the Empire of Rome. When Hannibal was a man, and ruled his father's kingdom, he waged war against the Roman enemy, for year after year."

Abraham was kneeling up now, listening excitedly.

"Did Hannibal beat the Romans? Did he? Did he?"

Istanbul: The Slave-Market

"In the end, Hannibal decided that the only way to defeat the enemy was to attack it at its heart. He raised a great army of soldiers, horses and even elephants, left Africa, and travelled for month after month, crossing great rivers, and then terrible snow-covered mountains, where countless men and animals died of cold. At last, he reached the Romans in their own land, but his forces were too small and weak by now. They fought bravely, time and time again, but in the end the Romans chased them away back home ..."

"Oh, *NO!*" burst out Abraham.

The little old Russian slave put his finger to his lips, smiling.

"Listen! Hannibal remembered the promise that he had made to his father, that he would never give in to the Romans, so that rather than be ruled by them, he left his home to wander the earth. And, in the end, he settled near the place where we are now, until he heard that the Romans had found him out, and were following him even here. So, rather than be captured by his old enemy, he took poison and died.

"But the story of Hannibal and his

elephants, and their march over snowy mountains to attack Rome, has never been forgotten. His grave is not far from here, and everyone knows it as 'Hannibal's Grave'. Think of Hannibal, Abraham, and what he suffered, and how he didn't give in to the enemy. He was an African, like you."

Abraham's gloom had completely lifted. "When I was little, I had an adventure with some elephants," he exclaimed excitedly.

"Well, you're not so very large now, but I think it's your turn to tell a story. What *did* you do with those elephants?"

So Abraham told the old cleaner of the Slave-Market the story of how a huge she-elephant, maddened by the pain of a spear-wound in her face, had led her herd up from the Wild Lands of Ethiopia to his home town of Dibarwa, and they had nearly ruined all their crops; but Abraham made them chase after him instead, so that the leader crashed down into a river-bed, and the herd had given up and blundered away again …

Abraham was standing up by this time, jumping around as he acted out how he had yelled at the elephants, and flapped his cloak and thrown stones at them, and how he had fallen over the river-bank himself.

"And my father took me to visit the Emperor in his Palace as a reward! He even told the Emperor that the story of what I did would never be forgotten, that grandmothers would tell their grandchildren all about it at their fire-sides."

Abraham stopped, and suddenly realised that the little group of black slave-children had left their fire-side, and were sitting listening to him, wide-eyed. He grinned at them.

"I bet *you* haven't got stories like that to tell!"

The children started laughing and cheering and talking all at once, and then they all settled down again round the fire, and took it in turns to tell their tales, while the old man swept the cobbles around them, and smiled as he listened.

As Abraham was falling asleep that night, he thought of Hannibal and his elephants and the high snowy mountains, and of how he never gave up.

Abraham Hannibal

I won't give up hope, Lahia, I promise. If I want to be free badly enough, I WILL manage it. I WILL be free.

But the days of waiting for a master were difficult. More slaves came in every day, and every day, slaves were sold, and every day, customers came, but no one bought Abraham.

Then, on the tenth day, a middle-aged Turk, short and stocky and weather-beaten and with work-stained hands, came in with a half-a-dozen guards and a couple of white officials in gorgeous robes and tall hats. They picked out Abraham, along with five other bigger black boys, felt their muscles and looked in their mouths and eyes, discussing all the while in their own language.

At last, they paid the slave-merchant after a lot of bargaining, took all six of the black boys, and led them out along steep, narrow lanes, the guards beating the crowds out the way with their fierce long whips, past two especially enormous mosques, and in through the biggest gate-house

Abraham Hannibal

Abraham had ever seen, into a huge courtyard, where the first thing he saw was a heap of human heads, their warm blood still steaming as it trickled down to soak into the grass ...

Chapter 6

UNCLE MUSTAFA

And so, in the Palace of the Sultan of Istanbul, the Shadow of God on Earth, and ruler of the world's mightiest Empire, Abraham began the strangest two years of his short life, and they were not unhappy years. There was cruelty there, but Abraham himself was kindly treated. This was a Palace far bigger and more splendid than the Palace of his Emperor in Ethiopia, even than the Palace of the Sun King, and Abraham never stepped outside it till the day he left forever.

A huge wall went right the way round the Palace, and inside the wall it was like a little city, a city of five thousand men, women and children, a city of secrets inside secrets inside secrets.

Abraham Hannibal

The courtyard that Abraham had first entered, where he saw the heap of heads of the Sultan's enemies, led through another great gate, the Gate of Greetings, to the Second Courtyard, where the general public could not go, full of fountains and flowers and trees, with huge stables and even huger kitchens, and the Great Council Chamber, gleaming with gold and precious tiles.

In these courtyards Abraham spent his time, for his work was to be a gardener's boy, and to keep the flowers and lawns perfect; but he could go no further, since the next gate was the Gate of Happiness that led to the Third Courtyard, where Abraham and the ordinary slaves like him were not permitted to go, except every now and then for some very special task.

At the heart was the most secret place of all, The Forbidden Palace, where lived the Sultan's three hundred slave-girls, where only the Sultan and the Black Slaves of The Forbidden Palace were allowed to go; it had its own gate in a corner of the Second Court, guarded by thirty Black Slave-Guards.

The weather-beaten Turk who had picked

Istanbul: The Sultan's Palace

Abraham from the slave-market turned out to be his new master, Mustafa, and he was a kindly man who loved his work. He directed more than two hundred gardeners, and in this world of dazzling magnificence, he was one of the few really down-to-earth, ordinary people, not easily impressed.

Mustafa spoke broken Arabic, and he slowly taught Abraham and the other new slaves to speak Turkish, along with all the skills of gardening. But out of all the slaves who took orders from him, he did seem to have a soft spot for Abraham. He called him Ibrahim, in the Muslim manner.

"I had a son once called Ibrahim, like you. My only child. You look about the age he would be now."

"What happened to him, Master?"

The gardener sighed, and looked out towards the eastern side of the Palace, below which lay the narrow stretches of water between their part of the great city and the rest.

"He was drowned," he answered quietly. "Together with my wife, his mother. Not far from here, just crossing the sea from the other side of the city. There was a storm blowing, but they wanted to get back home to be with me."

"I had a sister once, who was drowned," said Abraham.

Mustafa looked quickly back at him.

"Tell me about it, Ibrahim."

So Abraham told Mustafa the story of his mission from the Emperor of Ethiopia to the King of the Franks, and how his sister Lahia tried to go with him, and was drowned in the Red Sea; he told him how he and his friends were kidnapped by the raiders of the desert, about his Turkish master, Ahmet, and about the shipwreck on Goat Island, and the pirates on *The Star of the Sea*, and from then on Mustafa took a special interest in him, told him stories and listened to his. Soon, he stopped being "Master", and became "Uncle Mustafa".

As the months went by, Abraham became more and more used to the quiet routines of life and work in the Palace; his Turkish became quite fluent, and he grew taller and stronger, stockier too on the good Palace food. But having Mustafa as an uncle caused its own problems.

"When the call for prayer comes, Ibrahim, you always seem to avoid praying if you can. And

Istanbul: The Sultan's Palace

I've never seen you in the mosque, not even on a Friday. Are you not a believer?"

"I believe," muttered Abraham, looking at his feet. "But my prophet is Jesus Christ, not Mohammed."

"But we pray to the same God. Pray with me when you can, Ibrahim."

So, just to please "Uncle Mustafa", Abraham began to pray more often with the others in the Palace; but the words he said in his heart were always the old prayers to Mary and to his Father in Heaven that he had learnt long ago at home in Ethiopia ... though by now it was growing harder and harder to remember them ...

At prayer-time, as Abraham recited the prayers of the Muslims, his hand would always go to his neck, where his little silver cross should have been, the little silver cross he had been given when he was baptised at forty days old, in another country, in another life ...

I'm slipping further and further away from who I really am ... I wonder what they would think of me at home now, bowing and kneeling with the Muslims ...

It was a good thing having Mustafa on his

side. One alarming thing about Abraham's job was that many of the other gardeners were not ordinary black slaves like himself, or like the boys who had come from the Slave Market with him: instead, they were trainee White Slave-Guards, doing all sorts of heavy work around the Palace to harden them up before their army training - gardening, wood-cutting, guarding, kitchen-work, rowing boats and so on.

"You know, Ibrahim, there are hundreds of these young fellows round the place," said Mustafa, one evening after work, as he sat in a corner of the First Court, smoking his water-pipe.

"They never stay gardening long enough to learn how to do the really complicated, careful jobs that I'm teaching you boys, but ... my goodness, they have a very high idea of their own importance! They know they're going to be real soldiers soon, feared by everyone from the Sultan downwards. So, if one of them gives you cheek, or whacks you with his spade, whatever you do, don't argue back. It'll always be his word against yours. You could even find yourself in hospital, no questions asked!"

"I have a friend who was taken to be made

Istanbul: The Sultan's Palace

a White Slave-Guard," said Abraham. "Andrew is his name. He would never behave like that. Every day I look for him. It would be wonderful if he did turn up in the Palace!"

"He could be anywhere, Ibrahim. There are plenty of Slave-Guards, white and black, in Palaces all over the Sultan's Empire."

And Abraham never did see Andrew Robertson, though he never stopped keeping an eye out for him, just in case ...

What he did see was the real, grown-up White Slave-Guards ... and they *did* look fearsome. Some of them used to guard the First Court, and many more used to come to the kitchens in the Second Court every Friday to collect their rations in their giant food-pots, swaggering through in their coloured boots, long blue coats, wide baggy trousers and huge head-dresses which swept from high above their heads, right down their backs. Unlike almost all the other men, they didn't wear beards, but they had nasty long moustaches, which somehow made them look especially fierce; nearly every one of them went about with a permanent "Don't you get in *my* way" sort of sneer on his face.

Abraham Hannibal

One day, in fact, two of them walked right into Abraham as he was crouching next to a rose-bush that he was clipping, and sent him and his clippers flying; they simply laughed, and he didn't dare say a word. Mustafa had warnings about the White slave-Guards too.

"If you ever hear them drumming on those food-pots, Abraham, run for cover! It means they're not happy with something - food

or wages or some decision of the Sultan's ... and then there's no stopping them."

He lowered his voice. "A good few Sultans have met their end at the hands of the White Slave-Guards, you know."

"What does the Sultan have them for, then?"

Mustafa shrugged his shoulders. "I've sometimes asked myself the same question, Ibrahim. Probably there's some reason so old no one remembers it any more. There's a lot of questions you could ask about this Palace, and you wouldn't get answers to any of them."

Chapter 7

A VOICE FROM THE PAST

Life in the Palace wasn't all hard work. Abraham made a friend, Orhan, in the Palace Offices, who sometimes let him look at the precious books from the Palace Libraries – beautifully hand-written and decorated, like the ones back home in Ethiopia, not machine-printed like the French books that Doctor Poncet had shown him back in Ethiopia - and magical books they were too, with curly gold Arabic letters, and pictures rich with deep bright colours and pure gold leaf.

Orhan would sometimes give him paper and pens, and sometimes Abraham would have a go at copying a picture, or even drawing an archway or a window, and Orhan would watch over his shoulder and be impressed.

Istanbul: The Sultan's Palace

"You shouldn't be a gardener, Ibrahim! You should be trained up as a scribe or a book-illustrator! Maybe even as an architect!"

But Mustafa would quickly bring him down to earth again.

"Not a chance, Ibrahim, not a chance! Nobody changes his job here. You stay where God puts you, and that's the end of it!"

There were even lighter times, too. Often Uncle Mustafa used to take him to one or other of the wonderful steam-baths inside the palace walls, where for the first time Abraham felt how wonderful it was to flop in the hot baths and the icy cold baths and the steam-rooms where you nearly fainted from the heat, but all your aches and tiredness floated away. And his master had a surprisingly mischievous side to him, which, one day, led to a marvellous discovery.

Every now and then, the Black Slave-Guards used to come out of the Forbidden Palace and stroll in the bigger courtyards. Most of them were far too fat, and looked dreadfully unhealthy. They wore the most magnificent long robes, and the strangest hats, enormously tall and narrow.

Abraham Hannibal

One day, Abraham was planting out some seedlings in the flowerbeds in the Second Courtyard when Mustafa came by.

"You know why those Black Slave-Guards are so fat and ugly, don't you, boy?" he said, grinning.

Abraham looked blank.

"No. Why?"

"So that the Sultan's slave-girls won't fall in love with them, of course!" laughed Mustafa.

He suddenly crouched down and got very busy helping Abraham.

"Shhhhh! Here they come. Forget I spoke!"

Mustafa waited until two Black Slave-Guards swept past.

"You know, Ibrahim, I've just thought of something. One of those men is the Chief Black Slave. I have an idea that he comes from your homeland. It is Ethiopia, isn't it?"

Abraham's face lit up. "Really? I'd love to speak to him about it. Do you think I dare?"

Mustafa thought for a moment. "Get yourself washed, quickly! We'll see if we can catch him up."

Istanbul: The Sultan's Palace

They found the two men resting by a fountain. Mustafa bowed to the older, more grandly-dressed of the two. He was a giant of a man, tall and broad as well as fat, dark-skinned, though not as dark as Abraham.

"Peace be with you, Oh Most Gracious Lord!" said Mustafa.

"Peace be with you, gardener!"

"I have here a boy who wishes to speak with you about a certain land."

"Indeed. Then let him speak."

"Oh Most Gracious Lord ..." began Abraham in Turkish, since it seemed to be the right thing to say. And then he suddenly burst out in his own language, the language of Ethiopia that he hadn't spoken for so long.

"Greetings! I have heard that your home is Ethiopia ..." and then to his dismay, he dried, and more words wouldn't come.

The fat old man jumped, and stared at Abraham. Then he smiled, and, very slowly, started answering in the same language.

"Greetings, boy. You are ... from ... Ethiopia?" Then he shook his head, and said in Turkish, "It's no use. It's been too many years. I

have forgotten my own language. I think, my boy, that you have too."

He waved his hand at Mustafa and his friend. "Leave us, if you please. I wish to speak with this boy. Sit at my feet, boy. Let us think of past days. What do you remember of your home?"

So Abraham told the old slave about his family, and about his home, and how he came to leave his country, and then the old man told him about his childhood - he remembered very little - and how he had been captured by Arab raiders and taken north down the river Nile and then across the sea to the Sultan's Palace.

Darkness began to fall. The old man sighed.

"I must go back home now. Except that we have no real home, you and I. There are many like us in this Palace, little boy."

He shook his head sadly, and his flabby cheeks wobbled. "You are more fortunate than I, boy. I have great power and riches but ... only a little happiness, a very little. No wife, no children to comfort my old age. And now it is too late. *You* have your whole life in front of you.

Abraham Hannibal

Who knows what may happen?"

Abraham did feel sorry for the old man, but he was suddenly distracted by an idea.

"I know ... I think I know ... a girl in the Forbidden Palace."

The old man raised his eyebrows in shock.

"I know her from before ... she is from England. Her name is Elizabeth."

The Chief Black Slave-Guard gave a puzzled frown.

"She is about sixteen years of age, and she has golden hair and blue eyes," went on Abraham.

"Ah, yes! I know the one! She is beautiful. We call her Morning Star."

"How is she? Is she well?" asked Abraham anxiously. "How can she not be well? She is the most beautiful of the slave-girls."

"If I write a message, could you give it to her? Please?"

"Do not mention it to anyone, and I will do it. Have it ready at this time tomorrow. But now I must go back."

That night, Abraham asked Orhan from the Palace Offices if he could borrow some paper and pen and ink, and by lamp-light he drew a picture of himself with a spade and some flowers, and another one of Elizabeth dressed as she had been on the ship, with a chess-board next to her, except that he had to draw it standing up, so that you could see the black and white squares and work out what it was supposed to be. And with great difficulty, not at all sure that he remembered how to do it correctly, he wrote Abraham and Elizabeth underneath the pictures in English letters.

Two days later, he got his reply. It was a picture of Elizabeth in the kind of clothes she had been made to wear at the Slave-Market, with tears running down her cheeks, and her name. That was all.

Abraham did not try to get in touch with Elizabeth again.

It's hopeless! What can I do to cheer her up? We can't even write each other proper letters! It's just too terrible to think about.

But every time he saw the Chief Black Slave strolling in the courtyard, they used to greet each other in their own language and then Abraham would ask in Turkish,

"How is Morning Star, Oh Most Gracious Lord?"

And the old slave would smile and reply,

"She is well, my young friend."

And Abraham would feel comforted.

The months passed by. One of the worst jobs was when Abraham had to help with night parties. It meant going to bed very late, and still having to get up at dawn the next day, but that wasn't the worst of it. The worst bit was fixing the lamps on the tortoises. His Highness the Sultan, the Shadow of God on Earth, had somehow got the idea that it would be fun to light up night-time parties by having tortoises crawling through the flower-beds and across the lawns with little oil-lamps on their backs. The amount of work this involved was unbelievable.

Abraham Hannibal

First you spent the whole day, in between the other jobs round the garden, catching the tortoises and putting them in their pen. Then, in the evening, you had to take hold of them one by one and tie the fiddly little brass lamps on their backs with nasty stiff little gold ribbons that tied under their stomachs. If you put the oil in the lamp beforehand, most of it dribbled out when you were struggling to tie the lamp on, but if you didn't, it was a dreadful business trying to keep the tortoises still while you poured the oil into the little hole. Then you had to light the lamps with a nasty smoky kind

of skinny candle which kept going out.

At last, when it was properly dark, you could let the tortoises loose, and wait for all the guests to notice and start clapping politely. Well, it did look quite sweet, all these little lights wandering very slowly through the tulips. But then the poor creatures would get so nervous about all these strange goings-on that half the time they would refuse to move, or go and hide under a bush and knock their lamps crooked ... crazy, completely crazy...

There was only one tortoise, a big old one, who had any sense at all, and always behaved itself. It only took a minute to catch her and put her lamp on, but actually, Abraham often used to talk to her for a bit longer, since he had grown quite fond of her. He decided her name was Lucky.

Then one day, Abraham got news which made him feel quite different about the garden-party that night.

Chapter 8

TSAR PETER'S AMBASSADOR

Abraham reached right up to Uncle Mustafa's shoulder by now. In some ways, they were closer than Abraham had ever been with his own father - after all, the Lord of the Sea had always been so busy, and so important. It was dear Uncle Mustafa who passed the wonderful news on to him, very early one morning as Abraham was digging goat-dung in around the roses.

"Ibrahim, there's a Frank coming this evening, a very important one. Maybe he knows your Frank, that doctor, and can give you some news."

Abraham had whirled round and dropped

the garden-fork on his foot, but he didn't even notice.

"A Frank! A real Frank! Maybe I can get a chance to speak to him, somehow!"

But then a depressing thought struck him.

"Is he a proper Frank from the Sun King's country, or one of the other kinds? There's lots of different kinds of Franks, you know, from different places, and they don't even all talk the same language."

Mustafa shook his head.

"That one I don't know. All I know is that he's so important that he's going to be allowed into the Third Courtyard."

Abraham spent the hours till evening, when he was supposed to be getting ready for the garden-party, day-dreaming about the Sun King and his Palace and Doctor Poncet. To tell the truth, he couldn't remember exactly what the French doctor looked like any more, not so as to see him in his mind's eye, but he did remember that he was funny and kind and took a lot of trouble. And he definitely remembered his stories of the marvels of France and the Sun King's Palace.

Abraham Hannibal

"Mirrors twice as tall as me, Lucky, and stone images of men and animals that spout water into the air, machines that can make books all by themselves, banquets lit by ten thousand candles ..."

That reminded him that he was supposed to be helping track down all of the tortoises, not just chatting to Lucky. He hurried on with his work, but soon was muttering to himself, practising once again those French sentences that Doctor Poncet had taught him so long ago:

"My name is Abraham, and my father is a noble lord of Africa. The Emperor of Ethiopia sends brotherly greetings to the King of the Franks ... You'd better bring me luck, Lucky!" he remarked to the old tortoise. "Not like the last time I tried to talk to Franks and ended up on a pirate ship!"

At last the time came. Abraham washed and put on his best clothes: good-quality baggy cotton trousers, shirt and wide sash, with a fine red woollen coat over it all, and a turban wound round his cap. Mustafa let him off the job of releasing the tortoises so that he wouldn't get dirty.

Abraham stood behind one of the little clipped trees that lined the paths, near a fountain in the middle of the Second Courtyard. He was half-way down the main path that led across the court, so that he'd be able to spot the Frank coming in through the Greeting Gate, and have time to catch him before he disappeared out through the Gate of Happiness into the Third Courtyard.

Abraham waited. The great lords (no ladies, of course, in this Muslim land, no mixed parties here as in Ethiopia) came in with their trains of servants behind them, the long sleeves of their bright coats and waistcoats trailing next to them, baggy silk trousers flapping, tall turbans wound round high caps, chatting in the fancy upper-class Turkish that Abraham could barely understand, and all went out through the Gate of Happiness.

Then at last, the whisper went round, "The Franks are coming! The Franks are coming!"

Quite a lot of slaves were gathered in the

corners of the court, watching: they didn't get to see Franks very often, and it was fun to look at their outlandish clothes and wigs.

At last, the little group of men came through the gate and started walking across the huge courtyard. As they came nearer along the little path, their shining clothes and huge pale wigs glimmering through the twilight, Abraham's stomach jumped: at least they were dressed like proper Franks, like Doctor Poncet. He decided that the oldish man walking at the front, with the bushy black eyebrows and clever high forehead, was the chief, and waited for the right moment.

Just as the group of Franks came up to the fountain, Abraham ran out from behind his little clipped tree, bowed right down on the ground first, Turkish-style, and stood up. Then he gave a real Frankish bow, and, once again, made his announcement in the French language:

"My father is a noble lord of Africa. The Emperor of Ethiopia sends brotherly greetings to the King of the Franks."

There was silence. The Franks looked at each other, as if they weren't quite sure what they'd heard. Then the leader stepped forward, put his hand on Abraham's shoulder, and seemed to ask a question in French, which of course Abraham couldn't understand. Abraham repeated his sentences; the man rattled off some more French. Silence.

Then the man turned round and called to someone in his group. A young man in Turkish clothes came forward; the leader said something to him in French, and the young man came up to Abraham and started talking in Turkish.

"This great lord asks why you speak of Ethiopia and the King of the Franks, and how it is you know some words of French."

Abraham started to explain about Doctor Poncet and his mission from the Emperor of Ethiopia to the Sun King, and about being captured in the desert, the shipwreck and the pirates. The young man kept interrupting and asking questions, and stopping Abraham while he rattled off the translation to the group of Franks.

The Franks had all gathered round, listening and staring and whispering, every now and then smiling or looking astonished. Some of them even sat down on the edge of the fountain to listen. Abraham would have been embarrassed, with all these grown-ups, foreigners too, concentrating on him like this, but he was so caught up in his story, so anxious to explain it all to the Frank, that he didn't have a chance to feel shy.

At last the young translator said, "We must go through now to be received by the Sultan, but this great lord asks what you want of him."

Abraham slowly said, "Well, since I was taken away from Doctor Poncet and was made a slave, I have wanted two things. I want to be free, and I want to go to the King of France. I have to give him the message from my Emperor. As the great lord is a Frank, perhaps he can help me."

The young Turk laughed, and spoke to the rest of the group, and then to Abraham again.

"This great lord is not a Frank, nor are any of the others – at least, they are not from France, if that is what you mean. He speaks French, but he is a Russian. His name is Peter Tolstoy, and he is the ambassador of the King of Russia, his special messenger to the Sultan of Turkey."

Abraham Hannibal

Abraham suddenly felt sick in his stomach and dizzy in his head.

I was hoping for so much, and now I'm back where I started! I can't bear it! I just can't bear it!

Peter Tolstoy was talking to the translator. Then, through Abraham's dreadful disappointment, he heard the young Turkish man say,

"This great lord asks me to say that his King, or Tsar, whose name is Peter, has told him to find some intelligent young black boys here in Istanbul and send them to him. This great lord feels that you are a capable and interesting boy, and would suit Tsar Peter very well. How would you like to go to Russia?"

"Would I be free, or would I be a slave? Could I be a Christian, or would I have to be a Muslim? And would I be able to get to France? I *must* see the King of the Franks!"

The young man laughed again, spoke to Peter Tolstoy, and then again to Abraham.

"The easiest answer is the one about religion. Russia is a Christian country, the Tsar is a Christian king, so I'm sure he would want you to be a Christian. As for slaves - in Russia, they do not always have them quite as we do here in Turkey. You would be a paid servant in the Palace of the Tsar. One day, perhaps, the Tsar would give you permission to go your own way. And yes, it's very likely that, one day, you might see the King of the Franks. His Majesty Tsar Peter, whose people call him 'Peter the Great', loves travelling to different lands, and he would certainly take a favourite servant with him."

Abraham thought of the Sultan's Palace, his home for nearly two years now, and of Uncle Mustafa, and Lucky the tortoise, and even of his gardening that he had come to take pride in.

I've got used to this place now … Why does my life keep having to change? I keep having to leave my friends … I don't know where I belong … I even keep having to learn new languages …

But if I stay here, I'll be a slave all my life, I'll end up like the Chief Black Slave, except not as important - just old and lonely and sad. I'll never be a proper Christian again. I've got to be like Lahia, and take a risk. If I really, really want to be free, I'll manage it somehow. This has got to be the way – this is how I'll get to the Sun King.

Abraham Hannibal

He said aloud, "I would like to go to Russia, to the Great King."

The Russians, who were chattering among themselves, laughed and moved on to the Gate of Happiness, Peter Tolstoy patting him on the head as he passed.

Chapter 9

ESCAPE

But it turned out to be not quite as simple as that. The Sultan, who had never noticed Abraham in his life, decided, now that someone else was interested in him, that he didn't want to let this unusual young slave go. And Abraham's friend Orhan in the Palace Offices explained to him that, although the Sultan and all the Turks were being very polite and welcoming to Peter Tolstoy and the Russians, it was only because they had to be: a few years before, Tsar Peter had captured a Turkish city on the Russian side of the Black Sea, and defeated the Turks - unheard-of for the Russians to win a victory! There *was* peace now, of a kind, but relations between the Tsar and the Sultan were what you might call stiff - the Sultan was in no mood to do friendly favours to his former enemy.

So, no permission for Abraham to leave - and there was no way of leaving this great walled Palace unless you were supposed to. That was the end of it.

At least, it would have been the end of it, except that, a few weeks later, Abraham had an idea. He caught the Chief Black Slave as he was strolling in the courtyard one evening and greeted him, as usual, in their own language,

"Greetings! How goes it with my lord?"

"Greetings, my boy!"

"Oh, most gracious lord, I have a very, very great favour to ask ... a very, very great favour ..."

Abraham lowered his voice, mumbling up into the Chief Black Slave's ear.

"Is there a way you can help me to escape from the Palace? The Russians wish to take me to their country, and I wish to go. They've asked the Sultan, and he's said no."

The Chief Black Slave was very doubtful, very unwilling.

"I am a very powerful man, Abraham, but if the Sultan should discover that I have gone against his wishes ..."

He shook his head, and drew one forefinger silently across his throat. But in the end, he agreed to try.

"There is a small secret gate that leads from the gardens of the Forbidden Palace directly through the wall to the sea. I will arrange for a little boat to collect you there one night."

"But that means ... I'll have to go inside the ... the ... Forbidden Palace ..." stammered Abraham, shocked.

He thought of the hundreds of mysterious slave-girls hidden in there that no strange man was allowed to see. And then he thought, "Elizabeth!"

"My lord, if you can help me to escape, what about the slave-girl called Morning Star? Could you perhaps ..."

He broke off. The Chief Black Slave was looking horrified.

"Abraham, the slave-girl Morning Star is now one of the Sultan's four chief wives. Even now, she is expecting his child. What are you asking me to do?"

"I didn't know ... you never told me ... But maybe, could I see her, to say goodbye?"

"What a boy you are! I'll see what I can do."

The Chief Black Slave was as good as his word. He acted as go-between with the Russians, fixing up all the arrangements. He even worked out a plan for helping Abraham to say goodbye to Elizabeth.

"I was thinking just of hurrying you through the Forbidden Palace disguised as one of the Black Slave-Guards who work there, but if we're going to spend longer, speaking to Morning Star, one of them might recognise you. I've got a much better disguise. How would you like to be a girl for an hour or two?"

Abraham wrinkled up his face, and then shrugged.

"All right. If you show me how to put the clothes on."

Istanbul: The Sultan's Palace

The day of escape came. Abraham hadn't dared tell Uncle Mustafa, not because he thought the old man would give him away, but because he knew he would miss his "nephew" dreadfully. But he couldn't just sneak away without saying goodbye.

"It's my only chance, Uncle Mustafa," he said, as the old man sat miserably with his head in his hands.

"I'll miss you, too, Uncle Mustafa, I'll always think of you. But I don't want to stay a slave all my life, and never ever go outside these walls. And this way, at least I have a chance of reaching the Sun King."

Mustafa sighed. "I can understand. But it doesn't make it any easier for me."

They hugged each other tightly, and said goodbye. Abraham had one last little important job to do, and after that he went with his closed basket to wait near the locked Secret Gate of the Forbidden Palace.

It was nearly dark. After a little while, there was the sound of a key grating in the lock, and the Chief Black Slave came out. Somehow, he had arranged for all the Guards of the Secret

Gate to disappear for a few minutes. Checking carefully that no one was looking, he whisked Abraham inside the Forbidden Palace.

There was another locked door, and another, and another, until they came to a horribly narrow, gloomy corridor with lots of little rooms opening off it.

"This part is where the Black Slave-Guards live." And the Chief Black Slave hurried Abraham into a little room, very richly furnished with fine carpets and cushions.

"Here's your disguise," he said, handing Abraham a bundle of magnificent silks and velvets. "You'd better keep your own clothes too, to change into later. You can put them in that basket of yours."

So Abraham changed into a fine slave-girl's clothes.

"But there's so *much* to put on," he grumbled. "What's it all *for*?"

There were baggy trousers of pale pink silk, and over them a long see-through embroidered dress, and then a long tight waistcoat with huge trailing sleeves, and on top of that a long bright coat, and a scarf and a little

Istanbul: The Sultan's Palace

cap for his head, and little curly-toed slippers.

The Chief Black Slave grinned. "Very nice. Your own mother wouldn't know you."

"I hope Elizabeth recognises me!" exclaimed Abraham. "Otherwise we'll be wasting all this effort."

"Don't worry, Abraham," replied the old slave. "She has been warned."

They set off through the rooms and courtyards of the Forbidden Palace. Straightaway, Abraham could see Black Slave-Guards everywhere, standing by all the doors, and his stomach tightened with fear. But he tossed his long head-scarf round his mouth and chin, and not one of the Guards looked at him twice.

It was a magical place. The walls were bright with wonderful patterns of fruit and flowers and curly Arabic writing, all done in tiles of green and red and blue; everywhere were windows and skylights of finely-carved stone and wood and coloured glass, everywhere cushions and carpets patterned in rich reds and blues, everywhere fountains and pillars, domes and arches. The air was full of perfume, and the sound of bird-song ... everywhere, there were cages with nightingales singing.

There were girls and women everywhere, playing music, singing, combing their hair, smoking water-pipes, doing embroidery, chatting.

It was the strangest possible sight for Abraham, since he had hardly seen a woman or a girl since he came to the Sultan's Palace, and he had not seen a woman's bare face at all for two years, not since the Slave Market: any woman who worked in the normal part of the Palace, or needed to pass through, always had her face completely veiled. And here was room after room, full of unveiled girls and women!

At last they arrived at a small room; a fountain, set in one wall, was playing gently.

"This room was my idea," said the Chief Black Slave. "The noise of the water means we won't be overheard."

On a raised part at the back of the room, sitting on a big cushion, sat Elizabeth, sewing. She looked up with a cry of "Abraham!", quickly dropped her sewing and came over. She took Abraham's hands, and said, in quite good

Istanbul: The Sultan's Palace

Turkish "Oh, Abraham! It's lovely to see you! But how lucky you are! To get away from all this!"

"There are some good things here," mumbled Abraham. "Some kind people. I've sort of got used to it, and I suppose you will too."

The three of them went and sat on the cushions, and Elizabeth said,

"Tell me exactly how you're managing to escape, and all about where you're going!"

So Abraham explained why the Chief Black Slave was helping him, and all about Peter Tolstoy and the great King Peter of Russia. She listened eagerly and then said,

"Have you heard my news?"

"About the baby? Yes."

Only two years had passed since Abraham had last seen Elizabeth, but she had aged much more than that. She really seemed grown-up - not exactly happy, but very calm.

"If it's a boy, I'm going to do everything I can to make sure he grows up to be the next Sultan. Then, with me to give him ideas, we can make some changes here. Lots of changes, for the better! But there's something else. Something wonderful! It didn't help *me*, but I

am so happy about it. Guess!"

Abraham shook his head. "I give up!"

"When I saw that my lord the Sultan was beginning to love me very much, I asked him if my brother and my father could be found and set free. Your friend, the Chief Black Slave, helped to track them down. They are both back in England now."

Elizabeth sighed. "But I had to promise never to ask to be set free myself ... What's that strange noise?"

Abraham listened. "Thunder, maybe?"

But it wasn't thunder. It was a low, continuous drumming sound, getting louder and louder.

The Chief Black Slave stood up, listening hard.

"I'm afraid ... my children, I'm very much afraid that ..."

"That what?" burst out Elizabeth and Abraham together.

"It's the White Slave-Guards. They aren't satisfied with something – their salaries or food or working-hours ... That sound is them beating on their food-pots. It's their warning that they're going to go wild and rebel. The Sultan himself could be in danger, madam."

Drum-drum-*drum*-drum, drum-drum-*drum*-drum ...

The drumming was getting louder and louder, nearer and nearer to the Palace, with blood-curdling yells and terrified screams every now and then. Outside the door was the sound of frightened shrieks and cries and whispering, and little feet running this way and that, and the voices of the Black Slave-Guards, rapid and worried.

"Madam," said the Chief Black Slave. "You are as safe here as you can be anywhere. Let me take this boy to his boat, and then I will come back to look after you."

"There's just one thing, Elizabeth," said Abraham hurriedly. "I have a present for you. And for the baby, for the next Sultan. She's called Lucky, and she'll bring you both luck."

He rummaged under his boy's clothes in the basket, and brought out the old tortoise.

"Here you are. She eats any green stuff, but she loves vine-leaves best of all."

Istanbul: The Sultan's Palace

Elizabeth stepped back a bit in alarm, but then took the scaly beast in both hands.

"Thank you, Abraham. She's lovely. Welcome to the Forbidden Palace, Lucky!"

The drumming and yelling were getting louder every minute, and the Chief Black Slave was getting more and more alarmed.

"Quickly, Abraham! We've no time to waste! The boatman may lose his nerve and go away!"

So Abraham and the old man ran through the rooms and corridors and little gardens of the Forbidden Palace, through the clusters of bewildered and panicking slave-girls and guards, until they came to a big locked door.

The Chief Black Slave unlocked the rusty lock, and they went through damp and dusty rooms that hadn't been used for years, up steps and down steps, through more locked doors, and then across gardens and down and down and down, until at last they came to a little door in a plain brick wall. The old man unlocked that, with difficulty, and there, outside, tossed the dark waters of the sea.

Above and behind them they could hear

the terrible din of the angry White Slave-Guards, drum-drum-drumming at the gate of the Sultan's Palace. Across the water, they could see buildings on fire and hear the sound of screams. Just below them, swaying with the waves, was a little light burning, and they could just see that it was on the bows of a small rowing-boat. The boatman had not let them down!

"Well done, my man!" said the Chief Black Slave, as he handed the shadowy figure a bag of money. "There's more to come when I hear that you've finished the job."

And the fat old man helped Abraham step across into the tossing, plunging little boat.

"Good-bye, my boy! May it go well for you in Russia! You deserve to succeed!"

"Goodbye!" called Abraham in the language of his homeland. "Goodbye, and may God bless you always for what you've done!"

The boatman pushed the boat off with an oar, and began to row across the choppy waters, towards the lights of buildings and ships not far away.

All around them, the dark night was filled with the glow of burning buildings and the

Istanbul: The Sultan's Palace

sounds of groans and yells, and the drum-drum-*drum*-drum, drum-drum-*drum*-drum of the White Slave-Guards, beating, beating, beating on their food-pots ...

Chapter 10

THE JOURNEY TO MOSCOW

Nearly six months it took to reach Tsar Peter. Oh, Abraham was so tired of travelling! After the humdrum quiet of two whole years in the Sultan's Palace, when he never stirred outside its walls, never went anywhere, and life was peaceful, suddenly dreadful memories of all those weary, dangerous journeys long ago, through the desert and across rough seas, began to flood his mind, and even to fill his dreams. And this journey was the worst of all. How often he wished that he had stayed gardening with Uncle Mustafa!

Peter Tolstoy had handed him and two other slave-boys - just normal black slaves from the Slave Market, not from the Sultan's Palace - over to a fat merchant with the jaw-breaking name of Savva Vladislavich Raguzinsky - not that any of the boys could manage a name like that: they called him "Sir" to his face and "Savva" or "Fatty Savva" behind his back.

Fatty Savva was travelling all the way to Moscow, King Peter's ancient capital, and taking the three boys along with his normal cargo of cotton and olive oil. It was to Fatty Savva's ship that the boatman took Abraham, that dark night when the White Slave-Guards went on the rampage. And it was in Fatty Savva's ship that Abraham began that terrible journey.

First there was the sea, the stormy narrow passage north from Istanbul, where you sail with the dark cliffs of Europe to your left and the dark cliffs of Asia to your right, gloomy castles towering high above, guarding the way.

It would be easy enough, on a dark and wild night, to believe the sailors who, in days of old, told tales of those cliffs ... of those cliffs clanging shut and grinding together, crushing the little ships that tried to sail through ...

Then at last, you sail out into the stormy, foggy wastes of the Black Sea, a sea so wild and savage that, in the olden days, sailors called it "the Friendly Sea", to try and fool it into being kind …

Time and time again, in those storms, Abraham thought he was going to die, and he and the two other black slaves, Isa and Seke, huddled down in the hold, praying that it would all be over quickly.

And waking and sleeping, Abraham's mind was filled with memories … and questions …

*Drum-drum-*drum-*drum … What has become of them all in the burning city? Oh God! Look! There is Lahia, sinking under the waves of the Red Sea … Am I going to drown, like her? No, no! Please God, NO!*

At long last they reached the tall city-walls and towers of Azov in the south of Russia, that had once been the Sultan's, but was now Russian, and they unloaded their cargo, some of it to sell to merchants there, and some to take to Moscow in flat-bottomed river-boats.

Then came the long, slow haul up the

great river Don, sailing with the wind when there was any, and when there was none, the boys helped to pull the boats against the strong current, struggling along the bank with their hearts pounding furiously, knees and shoulders and every joint aching, the rough tow-ropes digging savagely into their chests, even through their clothes …

On each side of the great river, there was nothing but endless grass-fields, empty and wild, with the fear always of bandit horsemen galloping up to steal their goods and murder or enslave them all …

The summer faded fast, and a chilly north wind began to blow, colder than anything Abraham had known. Even Fatty Savva's Russian sailors and workers began to feel it, and wrapped up warm on board and when they were toiling on the tow-path.

Then something else began to happen that Abraham and the other boys had never seen before, stranger by far: a shining, hard, cold crust began to appear on the surface of the water, and in the morning, the blades of grass were often white and stiff …

One day, as the three boys were out helping to tow the boat upstream, their cheeks boiling hot and their breath panting painfully in thick white clouds, they saw their first snow. The little white flakes danced down lazily at first, just a few, but then started to fall thickly, and the hard ground was soon soft and white. The boys wanted to stop and feel it, shape it and throw it, but they couldn't stop, couldn't let go the tow-rope. But at least they could feel it cold on their hot faces, taste it cold and delicious on their tongues, and scrape and kick it with their feet.

Fatty Savva, who was walking along the tow-path, not to help pull, but just to keep warm, came over to the boys.

"What do you think of our snow, then, boys? First time you've seen it, I'll be bound! It'll get much worse, I can tell you that for free – a nice change from the jungle for you!"

The boys had picked up a little bit of Russian by now, from the men working on the boats, but never enough to answer Savva back with what was in their minds. In any case, even Abraham wouldn't have dared. ...

Abraham Hannibal

At the next little town, they left their boat, as the river was getting too full of ice to be safe. They rested a few days in a tiny, smelly inn full of fleas, and by that time the river was solid.

The journey continued, faster now, this time on horse-drawn sledges, racing along the smooth icy surface of the river, their little bells tinkling. But, oh! The dreadful cold! Pulling the boat was almost better, since at least they kept warm, but this way the icy wind pierced through the thick wool and furs they wore wrapped around them, and froze their feet in their boots and their fingers in their gloves ... The Russians taught the boys, when their skin went grey and dead with frost-bite, to rub it alive again with the cold, prickly snow itself ...

It was all right for Fatty Savva - he travelled inside a comfortable closed sledge, snug with hot-water bottles, candles, even books to read - but for the others, on the open sledges, the cold was the sharpest pain that Abraham had ever known. And although he had no clock, Abraham slowly became aware of something weird and unsettling:

Somehow – I can't think how – the nights are

longer here than I've ever known them ... there are fewer hours of light, I know there are ... Oh God! I'm so far from home! I'm so far from everything that makes sense! How am I ever going to get to France?

And there was always the fear of not reaching an inn before dark, before the horses wore out, when the only lights they could see were not the windows of friendly cottages, but the eyes of wolves, glowing yellow through the shadows ... waiting ... waiting ...

One afternoon, their journey along the frozen river Don brought them to the strangest of places - a harbour, frozen dead, where galleys and tall sailing-ships loomed through the twilight, trapped in the thick ice, while others, half-built, lay like monstrous skeletons between giant sheds on the river-banks.

"Tsar Peter's ship-yards," explained Fatty Savva. "First modern ships this country's ever had. All Tsar Peter's idea. They'll be down-river to the Black Sea in no time if the Sultan should give any trouble again. *They'll* give him a scare he won't forget! It's not for nothing that people are starting to call our Tsar Peter 'the Great'! New ideas and inventions wherever you look, beating his enemies to the north and the south, making Russia a force to be reckoned with … That's what we are now, a force to be reckoned with! Ha!"

And Fatty Savva stamped one huge furry boot hard into the snow, as if he was personally responsible for all of Russia's latest successes.

The icy white days wore on, and Isa, the youngest of the three slave-boys, grew sick of the smallpox. They stopped for two whole weeks in a village, and Fatty Savva flapped endlessly around the poky, airless inn, chewing his nails.

"Tsar Peter asked for three black boys, I promised him three black boys …What if I lose one? What if I lose the lot? Don't you DARE die, you monkeys! Don't you dare die!"

Abraham began to get his drift.

The Black Sea and Southern Russia

You brute! All you care is keeping in with Tsar Peter! What about us? We're losing our friend … I'm losing ANOTHER friend!

And then, in that filthy inn, Isa, the youngest of the slave-boys, died; but Seke and Abraham lived to continue the journey north.

The wide open grass-lands gave way now to thick forests, and at last they left their smooth, fast road, the frozen river, and the sledges skidded and bumped over the rougher ground, the snow-covered rocks and holes and bumps and dips of the so-called proper road, until they reached another river, and in a little village they celebrated Christmas, Abraham's first since he had left Ethiopia three years before.

And a little later, Fatty Savva said,

"Just one more day, boys, just one more day, and then we're in Moscow!"

Chapter 11

TSAR PETER THE GREAT

It was a clear and sunny day, though very cold. The sledges swept along the ice of the Moscow river, and suddenly far ahead, Abraham saw something gleaming in the sky, and as they came nearer, he saw it was tall white towers with shining tops like onions made of gold, and below them great white walls that plunged right down to the river banks.

They turned away from the river, and scraped their way through one of the city gates, along snowy streets paved with logs of wood and lined with little wooden houses, cheerful with carved decoration round the windows and roofs, until they came to a great open square, full of market-stalls and goods and merchants and horses and camels and donkeys and the confusion and din of buying and selling; at one end was the strangest church, a forest of red towers with bright scaly roofs in half-a-dozen colours, some shaped like onions, some like the twisted turbans of the Muslims.

In front of them were more high white walls, crowned with towers, and behind the walls the white towers with golden tops that Abraham had seen from far away. They were let in through a huge gate, and at last into the royal Palace, where their filthy clothes and boots, wet with melted snow, were taken away, and they all had the chance for a hot steam-bath, just like the ones Abraham used to have in the Sultan's Palace.

At last they were all kitted out in fresh new clean clothes, and Fatty Savva and some Palace officials took the boys to be presented to Tsar Peter the Great.

Except that they were taken into a carpenter's workshop instead. Abraham and Seke looked round in bewilderment. There were all kinds of fancy drills and saws, and beautiful, complicated things made or half-made

in wood. In a corner, hunched over a model of a sailing-ship, was a messy-haired man in dirty jacket and knee-breeches. In fact, there were two model sailing-ships: one finished one, and one that he seemed to be making, copying the other.

"Your Majesty," began one of the officials, "I have the pleasure of presenting ..."

The man with the ships jumped up and roared, "WHAT do you mean by interrupting me in my work? HOW DARE YOU?"

He was huge, absolutely huge, by far the tallest man that Abraham had ever seen. One of

his eyes was twitching with rage, and his face had gone all red. Seke, who was younger than Abraham, suddenly began to sob, desperately biting his lips to hold it in.

"SO, THEY'VE BROUGHT US CRY-BABIES FROM AFRICA, HAVE THEY?" bellowed the man. "That's not going to do me much good!"

He looked at Abraham. "You seem to have more sense than your friend! Or are you afraid of the Tsar of Russia too?"

Of course Abraham was, but he was better

at covering it up. He answered clearly and firmly,

"No, I am not afraid."

"What do you think of all this, then?" said the king, still loudly, but not quite as loudly as before, waving round the room. "And what do you think of Tsar Peter?"

Abraham thought, and very carefully putting the Russian words together in his mind first, he answered slowly,

"I like this things. I like very much. I like very much to … to … learn. And Tsar Peter, I understand why his name Peter the Great. You are very, very big man."

Peter stared at him a moment, and then burst out into a huge laugh. He suddenly grabbed Abraham under the arms, picked him up, and held him so that the boy's face was the same level as his own.

"So I'm Peter the Big, am I? Well, that's true enough. But, my boy, you are a big fellow yourself! As big as me, who knows? You have the heart of one of your jungle elephants!"

Suddenly Abraham felt a stab of dizziness, as a memory came rushing in from long ago: his father holding him up at head-height when he was only a little boy, joking at how much he'd grown.

Abraham might almost have wept then, but the sadness was jerked out of him as the Tsar suddenly turned him upside down, and held him dangling by one leg, jiggling him up and down until at last he turned him right way up again and put him down on the floor, gasping and dizzy.

"I like this boy, I like this boy. He has a good spirit. But he needs to learn more Russian to be useful. Get lessons organised for him. The other black boy ... well, give him a fine fancy costume, and he'll look very good as a page-boy with a flaming torch in his hand."

Peter disappeared off soon afterwards, some trouble about a war with a fierce northern people called the Swedes, as far as Abraham could make out.

The weeks went by, and every day a cheerful monk called Father Simon, with a huge bushy beard, and his long hair tied in a bun at the back of his head, came and gave Abraham Russian lessons - speaking, reading and writing.

Then Tsar Peter returned - the fighting with Sweden hadn't gone very well, but it could have gone much worse, and things were quieter now. The boy spent much of his time with Tsar Peter, learning to look after his clothes and his washing-things, and so on.

Better still was looking after Tsar Peter's pens and papers and maps and account books, his books about nature and about buildings and about machines, his drawing paper and his woodwork tools - all sorts of interesting things that were fun to peek at - and generally running around fetching and carrying.

It couldn't have been more different from living and working in the Sultan's Palace, where the Sultan, the Shadow of God on Earth, lived in a world apart, and Abraham never saw him, except at a distance, surrounded by his slaves and guards and officials.

Peter was quite likely to play mad, scary jokes from time to time, like when he'd turned Abraham upside-down, but he could also be kind and jolly and keen to explain things. For example, Peter himself showed him how the account-books worked.

"You have a head for numbers, a head for numbers, Abraham, my boy. I'll get that German who's supposed to be tutoring my damn-fool son to give you a few lessons in mathematics. The more people I have around me who know what I'm talking about, the better! Goodness me, here's a boy fresh from the jungle who could teach these idiot people of mine a thing or two!"

Peter's eldest son, Prince Alexis, was three years older than Abraham. He was from Peter's marriage to his first wife who, according to the gossip, he hadn't liked much. He didn't seem to like Alexis much, either.

Peter looked across from the account-books into Abraham's face.

"Tell me, black boy! What would you like to do with your life? What would you like to do when you're a grown man?"

Abraham thought just for a minute. It was hard to explain in a language he didn't really know properly.

"In Ethiopia, my father's country, there are only two ... works ... proper, good works, for a man. One work is farmer, and one work is … is … soldier. I always want … wanted … to be soldier, like my father. But I … I leave my father's country, and I learn new things, I also think about make things … pictures, buildings, machines, inventions. I like to make this too, if I can learn how."

Peter looked at him in silence for a moment and then said, "Is that so, Abraham my boy? Well, in Russia you can do both at once. Fighting *and* thinking. Let's see how you get on. And when you are older … who knows?"

He put his hand on the boy's shoulder and sighed to himself.

"Oh, Alexis, Alexis … if you could only learn from this jungle-boy!"

Chapter 12

THE PAGE-BOY AND THE PRINCE

Then came the extraordinary Sunday in late spring, when Abraham had some time off, and was outside one of the churches near the Palace, drawing it. It was quite different from the low, round churches that he just remembered from home: in fact, it looked more like a fortress. All the churches near the Tsar's Palace looked like that, very high, but narrow and solid and strong. Inside, all the space seemed to go up towards the roof, not sideways as in the wide mosques of Istanbul.

Abraham used to love looking at the paintings on the huge pillars inside the churches, tall saints and prophets from the

Bible, glowing with warm colours, or at the other pictures set in pure gold, on the outside of the Holy of Holies.

But this time, Abraham was concentrating on the outside of the church. He had drawn it from the front, the back, and each side, and now he was trying to draw a bird's eye view, the way he'd seen them of other buildings in Tsar Peter's papers and books. The trouble was, he had never really learnt how, and he was finding it hard to get right. He suddenly realised that a giant figure was standing behind him, looking down at his drawings.

"And WHERE did you get hold of that pen and ink and paper, my young African?" asked the Tsar, in his most dangerous voice.

Abraham decided there was nothing else for it.

"I have take them from you, Most Gracious Majesty. I think you have plenty, very plenty. And also, you like if I learn new things."

"OH, DO I INDEED?" roared the Tsar.

Abraham took a deep breath, and braced himself for a beating, but the Tsar just continued talking, in a normal, quiet voice.

Abraham Hannibal

"Well, in that case, you'd better learn how to do these new things properly! Let me give you a hand. Hmmm ..." he said, looking at the drawings. "Not bad, not bad ... and you've had no lessons at all, I suppose?"

Abraham shook his head.

The Tsar sat down on the nearest step, and made Abraham sit down next to him. (For a King, he didn't seem to mind roughing it - in fact, he positively seemed to like it.) He shook his head thoughtfully.

"It's a strange thing when a boy from the jungle who's never had schooling is better at the things I value than my own son is. You stood up to me from Day One, my boy. My own son has never done that in his life. He'd rather sneak off, keep out of my way, do anything rather than face my anger. I've struggled and struggled to give this country of mine a modern army and navy, but is my son interested in helping my work? HA! Can you SEE him attacking the walls of an enemy city? HA! And there YOU are, Abraham, wanting to be a soldier since you were so high!"

And he gave Abraham a thump around

the shoulders that nearly knocked him off his step.

"Then there's this drawing of plans: I've been trying to get Alexis to learn the basics for years. Building fortresses, defending cities! That's what we need skills in! He hates it. He'd rather sit with those long-beards, his priest-friends, reading the Bible."

Abraham couldn't catch every single word, but he thought he was getting the general idea. In any case, even if he couldn't understand all the words, he could understand Peter's mood. The Tsar suddenly jumped up and started striding around, waving Abraham's papers violently as he spoke. His voice was getting louder, and the whole left side of his face was beginning to twitch.

"In God's name, what's the use of the Bible when the Swedes are waiting to take over Russia! If Alexis were Tsar now ... well, he WOULDN'T be Tsar. He'd have been defeated long ago. King Charles of Sweden would be sitting on this throne here in Moscow!"

Peter took a couple of deep breaths and began to calm down.

Abraham Hannibal

"I'd like to show my son what can be done by someone who puts his mind to it. Be in my private sitting-room this evening."

And that same evening, Tsar Peter's conversation with Abraham had a result that shocked the whole Palace. Prince Alexis had been out all day, and the Tsar sat muttering and grumbling, half-reading a book about how to make coal-mines and iron-mines, waiting for him to return. He was in one of his small sitting-rooms, with his plump and cheerful second wife Catherine and their two little children - Peter, who was nearly two, and Paul, who was just a baby. Abraham and the little boys' old nurse were in the room as well.

Catherine wasn't actually Queen, not like Peter's first wife, Alexis's mother, since in fact she and Peter weren't even properly married yet, but as far as Peter was concerned, she *was* his wife, and his Queen too.

Abraham was very fond of Catherine: she

was a very warm person, and wonderfully solid and calm, unlike Peter. She had a funny habit of cuddling Abraham and giggling when he made particularly silly mistakes in his Russian; as she was soft and large, and wore a great deal of perfume, white powder, and frilly lace, he would emerge from her hugs sneezing and half-suffocated – but happy.

The kitchen gossip said Catherine had just been a servant-girl before Peter met her, but Abraham thought that was probably a good thing: perhaps that was why she was so jolly and motherly, not proud at all. And besides – she gave him hope:

If a servant-girl can become the King's wife in Russia, maybe there's a chance for me to make my name here …somehow … sometime … Little by little, I'll earn Peter's trust, he'll reward me, he'll let me get to France …

"Come and tell us stories of Africa, Abraham!" said Catherine. "His Majesty tells me you are an artist. Draw little Peter some pictures of strange creatures!"

So Abraham sat on the floor, drawing giraffes and zebras and elephants and lions for

the little Prince, and then he drew Hannibal the African leading a whole army of elephants, and wrote the names underneath them all in his bad Russian. Catherine came and sat on the floor next to him, with Peter in her lap, and they laughed and laughed at the funny pictures.

And Abraham told them in his broken Russian about how he once had a lion of his very own, and about the time he chased elephants away from his father's town, and all about how he had left Ethiopia …

Then the old nurse came and joined them on the floor with baby Paul, and told them all the story of the magic prince Guidon, son of Tsar Saltan, whose wicked, jealous aunts plotted to have him put out to sea in a barrel when he was a baby, but who grew to be a mighty hero and ruler of a fairy city. Catherine laughed and clapped and called to her husband,

"Oh, Peter, darling! Don't you think your black boy is like Guidon in Nurse's story! He was sent off to sea when he was small, just like

Guidon, and who knows what he might become! Maybe a hero, even a prince!"

Peter grunted rudely, but he did manage a smile. "Well, he hasn't got much competition from people around here! Most of my subjects seem to be half-asleep. At least the boy is eager to learn, unlike some I could mention. Hey, what's that I hear?"

And, with strangely suitable timing, Prince Alexis was shown into the room. He was thin and tall, though not as tall as his father, and he had an awkward, nervous way with him; his eyes were set too close together in his narrow face.

Abraham scrambled to his feet, and Catherine picked herself up heavily and sat down in a chair with baby Paul.

"Come here, boy!" commanded Peter. "I have something to show you."

The prince slowly stepped across the room, and bowed low in front of his father.

"LOOK!" roared the Tsar. And Abraham suddenly realised that Peter was holding out the drawings of the church he'd done that afternoon. Alexis took them, looking bewildered. There was a pause.

Moscow

"WELL? WHAT HAVE YOU GOT TO SAY?"

"I ... I ... don't know what to say ... they're drawings of the church ..." stammered the prince.

"OF COURSE THEY ARE! And do you know who did them? This black boy from the jungle, who's never had a drawing lesson in his life! He has more talent in his black little finger

than you have in your whole body! And his great aim is to be a soldier! How long have I tried to train you for a position of command in the Army?"

Peter's voice grew high and piping, like a silly girl's in a play.

"But you'd rather sit with your long-beard friends, reading the Bible while our enemies hammer on the gates of Moscow! Or worse still, you sit plotting with the long-beards, plotting to undo all my work!"

Alexis simply stood and stared at the ground; Abraham could see his narrow shoulders shaking, the drawings trembling in his hands.

Peter carried on, in his quiet, most dangerous voice.

"Go to your rooms, and show me what you have learnt. Draw me one building of your choice - front view, side views, back view, bird's eye view, vertical section. You have two hours."

The prince stood still for a moment, and then turned and went out in silence, still holding Abraham's drawings in his hand.

Catherine took a deep breath, and shook

her head.

"You are too hard on the boy, Peter. We can't all be like you."

"Be quiet, woman! You don't know what you're talking about! If that boy is to be the next Tsar, it's time he changed his tune. He wants to drag this land back into darkness, but I'm going to see that my kingdom is fit to be part of Europe, if it kills me. No, not just part of Europe! This kingdom of mine is going to *lead* Europe, lead the world! If not in my lifetime or my son's lifetime, then at least in times to come! AND ALEXIS IS NOT GOING TO GET IN THE WAY OF THAT!"

As Abraham watched in fascinated horror, Peter's face was beginning to twitch again, all down the left side. He gasped for breath, and his eyes began to roll. Catherine pushed young Peter into Abraham's arms and rushed forward to hold her husband, but his whole left side began to shudder; his eyes rolled back so that Abraham could only see the whites; his knees gave way, and Catherine could not hold him up: his huge body sank onto the floor. Little Peter started screaming, and the nurse ran for help, baby Paul tucked under one arm while she opened the door.

At last, everything was quiet. The nurse had taken the two little boys to bed. Catherine was sitting on a heap of cushions, and the servants had tugged and lifted the Tsar's huge body so that his head lay in her lap, while she stroked his forehead and softly murmured,

"It's all right, it's all right, my Peterkin. Everything's going to be all right. Just sleep. Sleep as long as you want."

The Tsar slept. No one thought to send Abraham away, so he simply stayed. After an hour or so, Peter woke up, and sent Abraham off for beer and bread and cheese. The scare was over - until the next time.

The Tsar and Catherine ate, and gave Abraham some too.

"Time for bed, I think," said Peter. "I feel as if I've just done a twenty-mile march."

At that moment, the sound of a gun-shot echoed along the Palace corridors. The three of them looked at each other, and made for the door. People were shouting and running up and down in confusion.

"It's the Prince's room!" said someone. And sure enough, when the first servants arrived there and opened the door, there was Prince Alexis, sitting white-faced at his desk, a bloody handkerchief round his right hand, a pistol in front of him. And also on the desk was sheet upon sheet of crumpled paper, with front views and side views, bird's eye views and vertical sections of buildings, all crossed out and scribbled on.

The crowd of servants at the door made way for the Tsar and Catherine to enter; Abraham peeped into the room as best he could.

The prince rose unsteadily to his feet.

"I'm sorry, Father," he said. "I was cleaning my gun, and there was an accident. I've hurt my hand. I don't think I'll be able to do those drawings for you, not now."

Chapter 13

PETER'S CITY

Winter really was over. It wasn't that the weather was properly hot, but the daylight seemed to last forever: for the first time in his life, Abraham found himself getting up and going to bed in daylight, whatever the Palace clocks said. From time to time, Peter continued to speak of the risk of enemies hammering at the gates of Moscow, but his mood was much more cheerful.

One day, as Abraham was brushing down and sponging the Tsar's winter clothes, and putting them away for the summer, the Tsar suddenly said,

"Haven't heard so much from King Charles and the Swedes these days, have we,

Moscow

Abraham? They had me worried back in the winter, but they seem pretty quiet now. Now that summer's here, I think it's time to move up to the land we've won off that ... that young bandit, Charles! Off to see my city, Abraham, Peter's own city!"

Peter's city. It really was. Saint Petersburg. Peter had won the land off Sweden, Peter had decided to build a city there, to spite his enemy, in freezing swamps where a tiny scattering of poor farmers and fishermen lived in sad little huts. Everyone said he was mad - behind his back, of course. Abraham had heard all about it from the other servants in the Palace. It was one of their main grumbles. There was a fat, loud-mouthed drunkard called Boris in the kitchens who never stopped talking about it.

"You just wait! We have to leave comfortable rooms and proper stone walls, and all our friends and relatives, and go and sit in a swamp all summer, in nasty rough little huts which keep flooding every time the river rises a foot or two. There's no farms or markets for miles around, so there's next to nothing to eat, and all day long, and half the night, there's the sound of hammering and sawing, crashing and banging. The place is one enormous building site, but it's the backwoods too. Wolves and bears just walk straight in and gobble you up! And they say he's going to make it the capital city of Russia! In a few years, he's planning to make all of Moscow move, all the year round, lords and ladies and shopkeepers and tradesmen - everybody! He's planning to rule the whole country from out of a swamp!"

All through the grumbles, Abraham never quite understood, with his wobbly Russian, why Peter wanted to do such a crazy thing. In the end, he asked Father Simon. His little question really started Father Simon off. Normally so jolly, he suddenly went serious, and his booming voice sank to an angry whisper.

"It will be a sad day, Abraham, when the Tsar of Holy Russia moves from this ancient city crowned with churches, to live in a place chosen by man alone, for reasons of worldly power. He wants to be nearer to the countries of the West - France and Holland and England - countries that do not share our holy faith."

"But those countries aren't Muslim - they

are Christian like Russia also, I think?" said Abraham, puzzled.

"Hmmph!" snorted Father Simon. "They call themselves Christian, but they are not Christian as we are Christian in Holy Russia! They are a godless lot, with no respect for old ways, always chasing after the new. And our Tsar is just the same, always chasing after the new. First men had to shave their beards off, then the old Russian clothes weren't good enough for him, and men and women had to wear new-fangled foreign clothes, then he had women coming out of the home, wandering around all over the place, mixing with men at parties! And new machines, and ships, and new subjects at school, and foreigners everywhere you look, and I don't know what-all. I tell you, Abraham, all these new ways of doing things have God's curse on them! And the Tsar's new city is nothing but Babylon – Babylon, I say! It has God's curse on it! How could it be otherwise? "

But the German tutor who sometimes gave Abraham lessons in mathematics had another story.

"His Majesty cannot bear to stay in Moscow

all his life. When he was a young boy, the City
Guards rebelled, and hacked many members o
his mother's family to pieces in front of his eyes
So Moscow is full of bad memories for him. He
wants to make a fresh start."

And Abraham thought of that terrible
night in Istanbul, the year before, when the
White Slave-Guards had rebelled and attacked
the Sultan's Palace, the night he escaped onto
the Russian ship.

*Drum-drum-*drum*-drum ... flames lighting up
the night sky ... What did happen to the Sultan, to
Elizabeth, to everyone in the Palace? Please God, no.
hacked to pieces ... Not like here in Moscow ... Imagine
Peter's family hacked to pieces before his eyes, when he
was only a boy ... Is that why he has those strange fits
of twitching and fainting? Poor Peter, poor Tsar ..
Peter the not-so-Great after all ...*

Chapter 14

FLOOD!

It looked as though Father Simon was right. The journey from Moscow to Saint Petersburg certainly seemed to have a curse on it. It took them over four weeks to travel the four hundred-odd miles, through wild forests and across marshes buzzing with mosquitoes, on horseback or bumping in dreadful bone-shaking carts, with more than twenty rivers to cross, not one of them with a bridge or a ferry. However you went, it was no quicker than walking.

And when Abraham arrived at the four-year-old city, he could well believe it was cursed: nothing but grey sky, and a great grey river flowing through grey marshes into the grey sea ...

Almost the only proper building was a fortress, and even that was only wood and earth;

as Peter and his followers approached it and the
little log cabin nearby which was his "Palace"
while he was here, they passed through crowds
of workers, their bony faces grey with mud and
hunger, grey with sickness and tiredness, their
ragged clothes and their hands caked with grey
mud, as they struggled to shift the soggy soil
without spades or wheelbarrows, digging
foundations and canals with their hands, shifting
the mud in their cupped hands or in the corners
of their shirts. Their homes were nothing but
the most dreadful shacks. Abraham's heart sank.

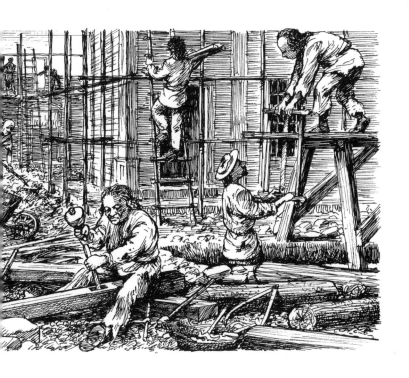

Has the Tsar gone mad? This can never become another Moscow!

But here and there were a couple of dozen reasonably solid wooden houses, even some grand ones belonging to nobles, and near Peter's little log cabin was a cheerful inn where they could have some merry evenings. And on the plans and drawings, the new city looked wonderful: canals, bridges and streets, shops and tall Palaces, gardens and churches, and statues everywhere. There would be parks with fountains and statues and little clipped trees ...

it all started to remind Abraham of something ...
Of course! The pictures of France and the Sun
King's Palace in Doctor Poncet's books! He'd
spent hours looking at those amazing drawings,
back in Ethiopia. He asked Peter about that.

"Your Majesty, in France, there is the Sun
King ... He has palaces and parks like these ... Are
you making a city like the Sun King's city?"

Peter laughed. "What do you know about
the Sun King, my young African? Well, in a way,
you are right. I am looking for the new ways of
building. This is going to be a new kind of city
for Russia. I've had enough of old Moscow. It is
full of bad memories for me. But here, my new
city is going to be Paradise."

Abraham nodded. He understood about
bad memories.

But then something happened that made
Paradise seem a long way off for Saint
Petersburg. One night, a strong wind started to
blow in from the sea, and blocked the great river
from flowing out - so it emptied itself sideways.

Saint Petersburg

The city was at sea-level, and it didn't take much to flood it.

The first that Abraham knew about the flood was when he was woken by a nasty damp feeling underneath him; he was sleeping on a mattress outside Peter's bedroom door in the little log-cabin, and as he felt around him, he found that it was soaked through, and the floor was awash. He jumped up and beat hard on the Tsar's door; he could see the water creeping in under it.

"Master! Your Majesty! Water! Much water! In all the house!"

Peter and his followers got themselves out and into little boats; they suffered wet feet, but nothing worse.

A fierce wind was howling in off the sea. The water rose fast, roaring and bubbling up from all the different branches of the river and the half-dug canals, rising higher and higher up the walls of the houses, inside and outside. Bits of hut, bits of building materials, even clothes and food, came bobbing higgledy-piggledy along in the rushing water.

Everywhere people were paddling their

boats along the streets, or huddling, wet and miserable, in trees or on their roofs.

"What a sight!" said the Tsar. "Look at them all up there, perching like a lot of birds!" And he laughed. "Isn't it a fine sight, men?"

At that moment, Abraham decided that he hated his master.

On one roof that barely poked up out of the raging waters, sat a young man, hunched and weeping.

"WHAT ARE YOU CRYING FOR?" bellowed the Tsar against the roaring wind.

"It'll all be over soon!"

"It's over already," came the man's thin, strained voice. "She's dead." And he opened his arms to show a little child lying on his lap. "Drowned ... drowned." And then he burst out violently, "I ... I ... curse this city, and I curse our Tsar who makes us live here!"

Abraham and the other men gasped and looked at Peter in panic, but he remained calm: there was no sign of one of his rages.

"I know that many have died, and will die, to build this city," he said quietly to those near him. "But it has to be. I will die for her too, if I must. Row on."

By night-fall, the waters had drained away. The log cabin was stinking and clammy. Abraham slept badly on his soggy mattress, and when he did manage to sleep, his dreams were filled with drowning and death: his father Fares the Lord of the Sea, sitting on the roof of a flooded shack, holding Lahia's body in his arms and moaning, over and over again,

"Drowned ... drowned ... drowned ..."

But when his father turned his head and looked at him, he had the face of Peter.

Chapter 15

KING CHARLES MOVES CLOSER

Much though Peter adored Saint Petersburg, he could not stay there for ever: it seemed as if the Tsar, checking on his huge kingdom, was never going to stay still: now he was heading south-west, towards Warsaw in Poland. They were like a little team: the Tsar, one of his favourite generals, some other army officers, a few ordinary soldiers, officials and servants – and Abraham.

The Swedes were camped to the west of them, and Peter had news that they were getting themselves ready to move towards Russia and real war - maybe planning to hammer at the gates of Moscow, as Peter always said they wanted to do ... or maybe, instead, to turn north, and attack Saint Petersburg, Peter's own city, built on land he had snatched from the Swedes in the firs place ...

That was when Abraham learnt of a new weapon he had never heard of before. Peter explained it to him, one night in a little country inn.

"What we do, boy, is to tempt them on Charles is a stubborn lad: he doesn't give up easily. Our army tempts them on eastwards across the wide empty plains of Poland and western Russia, harassing them at the edges, but never letting them get at us in a big stand-up battle. This way, we wear them out, little by little and don't risk our army. Meanwhile, they're getting further and further from home and friends, and from their supplies. And then we really hit them: scorched earth, my boy!"

Abraham looked puzzled.

"We burn the land ahead of them, all around them" explained Peter. "No crops in the fields, no harvest in the barns, not a cow, not a sheep, not a pig, not even a chicken, whichever way they turn. Starvation. We poison the wells, destroy the roads, the bridges, the towns ... anything that could be any use to them at all."

Warsaw

"But what about all the farmers, and the people in the villages and the towns? What happens to them?"

Peter shrugged. "They take their chance. It's war, after all."

And, sure enough, soon afterwards, Peter sent off horsemen to scorch the wide farmlands and forests of Poland, so that to their west, between them and the Swedes, all that Abraham could see was the red glow of the burning countryside, and thick clouds of black smoke swirling up into the sky ...

They spent a month in Warsaw, the capital of Poland, where Peter was trying to get people on his side against King Charles and the Swedes. Here the giant Tsar showed that he wasn't superhuman, after all, and collapsed from a fever. Abraham had never seen him so depressed and discouraged, and it was all made worse by some news from the furthest limits of the Tsar's empire. Abraham was at the Tsar's bedside when the messenger arrived. The Tsar read the letter, hit his head with his hand, and groaned.

"The Muslims in the far east of our empire are rising up against us. So are the bandits on the river Don. A whole Russian army has been wiped out."

He sat up in bed, and shouted out wildly,

"HOW CAN WE FIGHT IN THREE PLACES AT ONCE? How can I lead three armies? Are all my hopes for Russia to come to nothing?"

And he collapsed on his pillow, twitching and panting, while Abraham rushed to get him water.

Chapter 16

A NEW CROSS FOR ABRAHAM

Eventually Peter recovered; there was better news from the war with the eastern Muslims, and the little group set off north. By November, they were in the beautiful little city of Vilnius, far away in Lithuania. But here Abraham and Peter nearly fell out, badly, though it ended well.

It was a Saturday evening, and everyone was at a big, noisy dinner in a nobleman's mansion (most of Peter's parties and dinners were fairly noisy). Abraham was helping to serve beer and wine and vodka, but it was all quite disorganised, so every now and then he and the other page-boys could sit at a table with the guests and join in the eating and drinking.

Catherine wasn't with them in Vilnius; she

had gone to stay in Saint Petersburg, where quite a comfortable home had been built for them over the last few months, as she was having another baby. Peter was getting drunk: he usually drank more when she wasn't around. There *was* a queen there at the party - the Queen of Poland - but Peter certainly didn't listen to her the way he did to Catherine.

A band was playing a cheerful dance, and a little dwarf couple, a tiny, stocky man and woman dressed in magnificent ball clothes, were leaping and twirling to the tune in front of the Tsar's table. Peter was clapping loudly, slightly out of time with the music, and laughing himself sick; almost everyone else was clapping and laughing too, but not so as to drown out the Tsar.

Abraham had often seen dwarves at the Tsar's parties, as well as normal-sized jesters: Peter adored them and found them incredibly funny. He was just pouring the Tsar some beer when a messenger arrived. Peter opened the letter, read it, stood up (rather unsteadily) and called out,

"SILENCE! We have good news from Saint Petersburg. My gracious lady Catherine has had a child! A daughter, this time. We shall name her Catherine!"

There were loud cheers, clapping and stamping from the guests; the lady dwarf danced around, miming rocking a baby in her arms, while the man dwarf lay down on the dirty floor, waved his hands and feet in the air, and bawled loudly, baby-fashion.

Peter held his hand up for silence.

"Thank you! We'll all thank God for this tomorrow in church! And now, let's drink a toast, to baby Catherine, and to Catherine her mother! Good health to both of them!"

Abraham switched to making sure that everyone had vodka for the toast, and the guests downed their glasses in one, roaring out,

"TO BABY CATHERINE, AND TO CATHERINE HER MOTHER! GOOD HEALTH TO BOTH OF THEM!"

Peter suddenly grabbed Abraham by the shirt-tail.

"So, my young African! In church tomorrow morning! But hold on, hold on! Should you be there, I ask myself? A pagan black boy in church? Saying his prayers for my little

Princess? We'll have to make a Christian of you first! HEY, EVERYONE! Baptism tomorrow, for our pagan black boy! That'll be a fine first for Vilnius!"

Abraham simply stared at the Tsar. Peter wasn't much of a church-goer, but he had been in a church quite a few times when Abraham had been there too.

"Your Gracious Majesty, you know that you see me in church many times. I don't need to be made Christian – I am Christian all my life."

"NONSENSE!   Whoever heard of an African black who's been a Christian all his life? In any case, you were bought from Istanbul. If you aren't a pagan, you're a Muslim, like everyone else in the Sultan's Empire!"

In his mind's eye, Abraham suddenly saw the desert raider Kemal, his guard on the journey to the slave market in Arabia; he saw in Kemal's hand the silver cross he had been given at his baptism, he heard him spit scornfully, "Well, we're not going to keep *this*, are we?", and he saw his cross spinning off out of sight, far into the dust and grit of the desert. He saw himself as "Ibrahim", dressed as an Arab, then as a Turk, bowing to the holy city of Mecca five times a day, month after month …

Quickly, Abraham shut the pictures out.

"I AM A CHRISTIAN!" he burst out fiercely, "AND I DON'T NEED TO BE BAPTISED!"

Peter looked at him calmly.

"We'll see about that."

In spite of the beer and the vodka, Peter remembered everything the next morning. He went round collecting his servants and officials.

"SUNDAY MORNING! TIME FOR CHURCH, EVERYONE! Time to give thanks for my daughter! And I want to see my guests from yesterday! Off you go and round them up! Where's my little pagan black? Where's my young African? Abraham? Ready for your great day?"

Abraham stood, scowling furiously.

So, it really isn't one of his drunken jokes! He's serious. And there's absolutely nothing I can do about it!

Abraham Hannibal

"I shall be your godfather, boy! How would you like that? And I'm sure our graciou lady, Her Majesty of Poland, will be delighted to stand as godmother. How about that, then - roya godparents for our little black slave-boy! A fine joke, eh! Not to say an extraordinary honour!"

Abraham began to hesitate. Well ... thi *was* a bit different, then, from his christening a a tiny baby, which he couldn't even remember in a country far away ...

A King and a Queen as godparents, to welcom me to my new life in Russia ... If only he'd behave a though he meant it as an honour, instead of teasing m the way he does ... Sometimes he can make me feel I'n really worth something, and the next minute he's doing his best to make me feel like one of his dwarves .. Anyway, what choice have I got?

So Abraham went along with the grea crowd of last night's guests trooping off to the church, a good many of them looking the worse for last night's drink. The Russian church in Vilnius was only a little one, since most of the local people went to their own churches. Peter led the way in, with the Queen of Poland as an honoured guest, and as many of the others a could fit squashed inside, with the rest overflowing onto the street. Inside and out there was a terrible din of chattering and laughing: it all seemed to be a big joke. Certainly Peter was in jolly mood.

"Well, good people!" he roared. "It's not often in Vilnius you get to see an African jungle-savage brought into Holy Mother Church! It'll be a fine sight, I promise you!"

The priest had been warned about the baptism, and had a great silver basin of water ready for the ceremony, and a long white robe for Abraham.

"Does the black boy understand what he is doing?" he asked the Tsar. "Does he speak any Russian?"

"I DO speak Russian," cut in Abraham, which made the priest raise his eyebrows, shocked at his rudeness. "And I understand that I am doing this at the Tsar's command, but I am baptised Christian already in my own country, but His Majesty will not believe it."

The priest looked even more shocked, but he said,

"Will you put on the white robe to show

that you are entering into a new life o
holiness?"

Abraham pulled it on over his clothes. A
small choir began to sing; the chattering died
down, and the priest began to chant, not in
normal Russian, but in the old language of the
church, which Abraham knew was used for al
the prayers - just as in Ethiopia, priests used
a special old language when they prayed.

The Tsar and the Queen of Poland moved
beside Abraham to take their part, and the pries
asked them in Russian,

"What name is he to take?"

"Oh, let him take my name. Christen him
Peter."

Abraham could not believe that he had
heard right.

"You can't do that! I ... I ... mean, Your
Gracious Majesty, that's impossible. My name i
Abraham. I can't be christened Peter ... with
respect to your name, sir!"

"Nonsense, boy! Peter's a name you can
be proud of! You should have a good saint's
name, like a proper Russian. What kind of name
is Abraham, anyway? Some sort of pagan Jewish

Muslim nonsense! We can't have a Russian called that!"

"MY NAME IS ABRAHAM! I was baptised with it in my own country, and you can't make me change it! It's in the Bible! Isn't the Bible good enough for you? I won't be called Peter! WON'T BE CALLED PETER!"

Abraham started pulling the white robe off over his head and off his arms, panting and clumsy with rage. The church was quiet now, and everyone stared.

"You can't make me! I won't let you! My name is Abraham, and I won't ever change it! I am as good a Christian as you are ... Your Majesty ... and my baptism was as good as yours! I am who I am, and you can't make me into somebody else!"

He finally got the robe off, and threw it down onto the floor. He took a deep breath, and then stared calmly up at the Tsar, arms folded across his chest.

"I want to leave this church now. And I want to leave your service. You cannot force me to stay. I may be a servant, but I can leave if I wish."

The church was deathly quiet. Peter stood, his face expressionless, his arms folded too. For a minute, then two, the giant Tsar and the young boy stood, looking each other in the face. Then Peter bent down, picked up the white robe, and straightened it out. He held it out to the boy.

"Will you be christened with your own name, Abraham, with me and Her Majesty of Poland as your godparents, as a sign that you are part of my family, and that I will be like a father to you?"

Abraham gasped. A great sob rose inside his chest, and tears pricked behind his eyes. He controlled them both: why be weak now, when he had been so strong?

I've won! I've won! They're not taking my name away!

For a moment he could not speak; then he said,

"Most Gracious Majesty, I agree with what you ask."

And so for the second time in his life, Abraham was baptised with water, and for the second time he had a blessed cross tied round

his neck. Then he was anointed with holy oil
and then the service of thanksgiving for the baby
Princess Catherine began.

A couple of weeks later, they set off for
Saint Petersburg, to see the two Catherines for
themselves. But it was not the joyful meeting
they had been looking forward to.

Chapter 17

DEATH IN THE PALACE

As the Tsar's horses and baggage-waggons and sledges blundered through deep snow along the bumpy, pot-holed main road to Saint Petersburg, messengers came galloping towards them as best they could.

"Your Majesty, we have a letter from Her Ladyship, Catherine. It is ... it is important."

Peter tore open the letter, glanced at it, and quickly shouted out to his followers,

"We carry on at our fastest pace. My son Paul is very sick."

The rest of the journey was a desperate, panicky battle against snow-drifts and blizzards, the long hours of darkness, the bitter cold - a miserable struggle to reach home before it was too late.

Abraham Hannibal

At last they reached Saint Petersburg, and burst into the house. Peter leapt up the stairs three at a time to the children's nursery. Abraham wasn't at all sure whether he was supposed to follow, but he did anyway. As he peeked round the door, he saw the Tsar kneeling on the floor in front of Catherine, his head bowed, his hands on her knees. She was white faced, except for deep shadows under her eyes, and she sat rocking a flushed and restless baby Paul in her arms. Little Peter whimpered miserably in his cot, while the old nurse sponged his hot and aching head.

Over and over again, the Tsar was moaning,

"My sons! My sons! My sons! Please God not both my sons! Please God! Not both my sons!"

Baby Paul died that night. His father took him in his arms, the giant of a king holding the little body tight, their two faces pressed together. He walked back and forth across the room, again and again, rocking the baby from side to side, until at last Catherine made him put him back in his cradle for the priests to pray over him.

The hours ticked slowly by. The Tsar barely spoke, but sat at little Peter's side, or paced up and down the room, chewing his knuckles and his finger-nails as the boy whimpered and fidgeted unhappily, his little face sometimes hot and fiery pink, sometimes grey and clammy.

Two evenings after baby Paul had died, Abraham was curled up quietly on the floor in a corner of the nursery, watching and waiting. The Tsar was sitting by the cot, with Catherine next to him holding little Peter in her arms. Suddenly Catherine looked up from the little boy and quietly said, "He has gone."

Peter gave a great moan, and stumbled up from the bedside, and across the nursery. Abraham saw him suddenly strike his head so hard against the wall that he went into the worst fit that he had ever seen him have, collapsing on the floor, moaning and shuddering and twitching. Catherine knelt next to the Tsar, but she could do nothing to calm him: she herself was weeping, sobbing and shaking uncontrollably.

Abraham Hannibal

At last, when Peter's fit had passed and he could walk again, he staggered to his room, and shut himself up alone. Catherine went and tried the door; it was locked. She tapped on it. No answer. She tapped again.

"My lord! Can I get you something? Some food? Something to drink? Can I help you in any way?"

But there was no answer, not that day, nor the next.

Russia was without its Tsar.

At last, after three days, the Tsar's councillors and Catherine all gathered round his bedroom door, and the Chief Minister knocked and knocked again.

"Your Majesty! Your Majesty! We beg you to come out! Russia needs you! Will you force us to break down the door?"

At last there was the sound of the key turning in the door. Peter stood there, pale, unshaven, red-eyed, swaying slightly as he gripped the door-post. Abraham, peeping from the back of the crowd, saw him stare at the councillors blankly.

"What d'you want? I'm resting."

Saint Petersburg

"Your Majesty, Russia is lost without her leader. Everything is falling apart because of this sorrow of yours. The country's out of control. No-one knows what to do, without you to tell them."

Peter stood silent for a moment, and then said quietly,

"You're right, of course."

He went over to Catherine and hugged her gently. "We've been grieving too long. There's no use complaining about God's will. And we have little Catherine. Let's remember that."

Chapter 18

KING CHARLES MOVES CLOSER

Peter threw himself into supervising the endless building works in "Peter's city", rushing round checking the city walls against a possible Swedish attack, and planning a huge ship-building programme for the next year. However cold it might be, there he was slaving away with his workmen, always with a shovel or a hammer in his hand.

"Hard work's the best medicine for grief, boy!" he'd shout to Abraham. "Best medicine for anything, in fact!"

A little later, very quietly, he married Catherine. He did not call her his wife or his Queen publicly: too many people didn't approve of how Peter had got rid of his first wife, Alexis's mother, by forcing her to become a nun. And of course, Catherine *had* once been just a servant-girl: not quite the origins expected from the Queen of Russia!

But it was a happy time all the same: baby Catherine was well, Peter was always happier with his wife at his side, and then they made the long and difficult journey to Moscow, to spend a family Christmas there all together. A quiet Christmas it was, though, without the boys.

In Moscow, too, Peter had ordered the city walls to be hugely strengthened, and they went to inspect progress. It was like a vision of hell: thousands upon thousands of men slaving in the icy winter gloom to build up earth walls outside the old brick ones of the city, their breath gasping in thick white clouds, huge fires burning to warm and soften the rock-hard frozen ground, so that they could at least dig out lumps of earth. If the Swedes *did* come and hammer on the gates, Moscow would be well-protected!

And, in the horrors of the Moscow winter, when Abraham's bones ached from the cold, and his nose and fingers and toes felt as if they would drop off, he sometimes thought of the grey, bony, workers they had left behind in Saint

Petersburg, and their poor grey shacks, trapped in the middle of their frozen river and frozen marshes, at the edge of a frozen sea, and said a prayer of thanks that at least he didn't have to be there - and another prayer, for all the poor souls who did. And the baking hot summers and mild winters of the Sultan's Palace in Istanbul seemed very far away and long ago, as if the warmth and comfort of his old home were just a dream ...

The only thing that spoilt this time of new hope was the whispers: whispers from round the country, brought in by Peter's Secret Police, of how much the people and the nobles hated the new ways, the new taxes, the forced work on Saint Petersburg or in Peter's ship-yards and mines and factories ... whispers that, one day, the Tsar would find that he had gone riding around alone in the dark just once too often, and would find himself missing his head ...

And not long after Christmas, there was news from abroad that ended all chance of rest ...

A messenger came galloping in on the road from Poland. Peter, Abraham, two other pages, and a skilled carpenter, were all working in Peter's favourite place: the private carpentry workshop in his home. Peter tore open the letter, from one of his generals. He was silent a moment, and then said, quite calmly:

"King Charles and the Swedes are marching eastwards across Poland against us. Forty-six thousand men! They've crossed one big river already - that's one of our defences down between them and Moscow. Well, it's happening at last! At least we can get it over with now, one way or the other."

"You mean, there's going to be a big battle? A real one?" asked Abraham, in excitement. "We're finally going to wipe out those Swedes?"

Peter laughed, but without much warmth.

"God willing, yes. I wish it was going to be that easy, you young hot-head! But I fear we're not ready, not ready. Charles has one of the finest armies in Europe, if not *the* finest - superbly trained and equipped - while I have ... just an inexperienced rabble I've been trying to lick into shape only these last few years. Push them too far, and they'll just panic and turn tail. His army is modern ... ours still has a long way to go. Our cavalry bothers me, in particular. They don't have the control, they don't have the staying power ..."

Abraham's brain was whirling with hope and excitement.

A real battle! A real battle with Russia's most dangerous enemy! Now's my chance! If I can only prove myself as a soldier - maybe save the Tsar's life, or capture a Swedish general ... Then he'll reward me, give me my freedom, help me go to the Sun King ...

"Your Majesty, I'll do anything you want in this war. Just tell me where you want me to fight, what you want me to do ... I'll fight in the front line, anything!"

The carpenter and the other page-boys were looking on in astonishment at Abraham's eagerness. The Tsar laughed.

"We've got enough inexperienced country boys as it is in our army. You're untrained, and very young still. I think the best job for you would be drummer-boy."

"*Drummer-boy*! How can I win fame as a *drummer-boy*? I'm not a boy any more, I'm nearly a man now. I want to be a real soldier like my father, I want to fight, I want to become an officer, I want to do great deeds ..."

Peter swung round on his stool, and took hold of Abraham's hands.

"Hey, hey, HEY! What's all this 'I want, I want!'? Black boy, you came here from Turkey as a slave, remember? You've done very well for yourself, so far. Drummer-boy is fine to start with! That's how *I* started, when I was about your age! Do that job well, and who knows where you'll finish! Listen: just to cheer you up! I'll put you in my star regiment, the one I founded myself. You'll be drumming alongside me, wearing the same uniform - just a few sizes smaller, that's all!"

Abraham tried to smile, and said stiffly.

"I will do my best in this, as in everything you command me to do."

The Tsar smiled at him.

"You're a better Russian than many of my countrymen, my young African! I'd like to take your enthusiasm and give it to my soldiers by the bottle-full!"

Abraham felt his face grow hot with pleasure at the compliment, but that night in bed, he lay awake thinking about it.

Abraham Hannibal

A better Russian than the Russians, he said ... Am I really a Russian now? Is that what most Russians would call me? I bet they wouldn't ... They call me Tsar Peter's African, that's what they call me.

... I don't even know if I WANT to be a Russian ... Why do I want to fight the Swedes for them, then? I guess to make a name for myself ... because if Abraham is Somebody, it doesn't matter so much if he's a Russian or what he is. Because if I'm not a Russian, what am I? Am I still an Ethiopian, when I can't even remember my own language ... when I'm never, ever going to see my home again? How could I? A black boy travelling on his own through the Sultan's Empire! It can't be done!

He had never thought about it so clearly before, but that night, it hit him:

That's it. Somehow, I'll make it to France, and I'll deliver my message to King Louis, but I'm never going to see Ethiopia again. This is going to have to be my home. And I've got to make the most of it.

Chapter 19

THE SWEDES MOVE SOUTH

At first, this war with King Charles of Sweden seemed nothing but stop-start, stop-start; after all, it had had already been going on, stopping and starting, for eight years. And even when things *were* moving, it was often very slowly: fifty miles in one week was good going for an army.

It was definitely all much too slow for Abraham.

Aren't I ever going to get a chance to prove myself? What we need is a battle, but Peter's always so cautious!

And then the Swedish army ground to a stand-still again, and rested for two months, waiting for grass to grow for their horses. They had a hard time of it, though, with a countryside bitterly cold, and almost empty of food; and the country people round about quickly grew to hate the foreign soldiers in their yellow-and-blue uniforms, forcing their way into their tiny farms demanding on pain of death that they hand over their secret stores.

Abraham started a new job. Along with keeping the Tsar's things clean and tidy, he used to take turns with the other young page-boys acting as the Tsar's secretary: his Russian had got good enough by now.

The worst bit was when Peter suddenly had a bright idea in the middle of the night – and he was always having bright ideas – and scribbled it on slates with chalk by the light of a little lamp. *That* was difficult to puzzle out the next morning and copy up in best! In tents and inns and Palaces and huts, Abraham would sit and write up the Tsar's instructions and plans. Peter used to tease him about it.

"So, my young African! I bet you never thought back in your jungle that you'd end up writing laws for the Tsar of Russia! Not bad for a little black slave boy, eh?"

On The Move

Actually, Abraham wasn't so little any more: he was growing taller and broader, though he was still not full-grown – and of course, next to the Tsar, no-one looked tall. But he *was* pleased to be a secretary to Peter.

This is one up from being a page-boy … he must really trust me … One day, I'll somehow make my name, and I'll be free, I'll get to France at last, I'll find the Sun King. He'll see what us Ethiopians are made of!

Peter was able to go to Saint Petersburg for Easter, and cheer himself through another bad fever by ordering flower-seeds, cuttings and baby trees, and song-birds by the thousand, to beautify his new city. He even found enough energy to order all the nobles from Moscow to come to Saint Petersburg and start building Palaces there: the Big Move was really beginning.

But while Peter was in Saint Petersburg with Catherine, something happened that brought his fever back, and had him in bed till

he heard that the Swedes were on the move
again, and he dragged himself up to face them
baby Catherine died. Three children, he and
Catherine had had so far: three children, and
three deaths.

The Swedes started marching east in June
It was a wet summer. The horses suffered
horribly, struggling to drag cannons and
waggons through the mud, falling dead with
exhaustion and hunger. The soldiers were
ragged, sick and hungry, and time and time
again, they sank up to their waists in the thick
mud as they marched. A whole extra division of
their army was supposed to be coming down
from the north with plenty of supplies, but i
didn't arrive ... and still it didn't arrive.

But all the same, the Swedes managed to
cross the last of the big rivers between them and
Moscow. Now it was only three hundred miles to
go, with no barriers in between!

The Russian camps were full of legends

about the blond young Swedish king: how he'
been killing wolves and bears single-hande
since he was a little boy; how he'd crowne
himself king when he was fifteen, first led a
army into battle and victory when he wa
eighteen; how he knew neither fear nor love ...

Tsar Peter had a black-and-white pictur
of King Charles; Abraham used to stare at tha
hard young face, and wonder what made him
dare lead his little country against the huge mas
of Russia ...   King Charles started to fill hi
dreams at night ...

*That's him over there, rearing up on his stallio
at the head of his troops, his sword flashing and slicin
... isn't he young! What cold blue eyes ... cold and har
... He doesn't know what fear is ... No armour at al
... nothing to protect that blond head, his chest or hi
back ... I'll gallop up and force him to fight me in singl
combat ...*

It was a dream that Abraham started t
have again and again: Abraham and Charle
always fighting, the battle roaring around them
but the two of them in single combat, rearin
and wheeling on their horses, their sword
thrusting and clanging, until at last Charles fel

On The Move

bleeding on the battlefield, and Abraham triumphantly showed Peter the body of his defeated enemy ...

Now that the Swedish army had crossed the last of the big rivers that lay between them and Moscow, Peter knew what orders to give to stop them marching further. As the Swedish soldiers looked eastwards, across the flat plains ahead of them, they saw what Abraham had seen in Poland the year before: the red glow of burning fields, forests and villages, the sky heavy and black with smoke. This time, Peter's soldiers were not scorching the earth of a foreign people – they were laying waste their own land.

Between King Charles and Moscow, his heart's desire, lay a huge new desert, with not a blade of grass for his horses, nor a grain of wheat for his men. And he knew that northwards, the way to Saint Petersburg was no better.

Charles waited, and waited. And still the other part of his army, with its baggage-waggons loaded with food and uniforms, ammunition blankets and medicines, did not arrive. But go back was something Charles would never do.

And so, in the end, as autumn wa approaching, Charles went the only way left south. Away from Moscow, away from Sain Petersburg, further and further away from Sweden and Sweden's friends - but at leas towards farmlands that had not been burnt, and barns that had not been emptied of food.

And, at last, the extra Swedish baggage waggons came, slowly rumbling down from the north, but this time the Russians did strike - and destroyed the lot.

Chapter 20

THE COLDEST WINTER

The Swedes settled into a cluster of small towns and villages in the rich, fertile south; here at least there was still food in the sheds and barns. The Russians set up their own winter headquarters in a curve of small towns between the Swedes and the way to Moscow.

As autumn gave way to winter, the two armies waited. For once, Peter decided to take the lead: time and time again, he sent out small groups of horsemen dashing across the frozen rivers and streams to harass the edges of the Swedish camps and tempt the Swedish soldiers out. Each time, the Swedes found that the Russian army simply melted away; there was no battle, and they had left their firesides for nothing, all ragged and weak as they were.

At last, in December, the whole Swedish army were tempted out from their camps onto the open road, hoping to catch the Russians by surprise. But instead, the Swedes found themselves facing a new and unexpected enemy all over Europe, that winter was the coldest in living memory.

The river Thames froze in London, the river Seine in Paris, so that horses and wagons could pass across. In the Palace of the Sun King, wine turned to ice at table, and the nobles forgot fashion, muffling themselves up in thick cloaks and furs, huddling round huge log fires that could barely warm the vast and splendid rooms.

Reindeer and boar froze to death in the forests, cows and sheep in the fields, rabbits and weasels in their holes; squirrels and birds fell dead from the trees.

Windmills were frozen stiff and would not turn, so that wheat could not be ground for bread, and people died of hunger as well as cold.

In the huge, empty, windswept plains to the south of Russia, it was far worse still: there are no mountains, no barriers at all, between you and the North Pole, and the icy winds come blasting straight from the Arctic Ocean.

In December, Peter tempted the whole of Charles's army out into this freezing hell, leaving them stranded in the howling white wastes to fight a ghost army that vanished before them. For three days, the Swedes struggled to get back through the narrow gates of the towns, freezing stiff as they sat on horseback or in waggons, dying of cold as they marched, or surviving only to lose their fingers and toes and noses to frostbite.

Even Abraham thought Charles had been foolish to risk his men so needlessly, and he was not sorry to stay indoors: as he peeped through the little double windows of their inn at the murderous whiteness outside, a snow-storm blasting fiercely up and down the alley-way, he often thought of the story he had heard so long ago, in the Slave-Market at Istanbul, about the young African general who, once upon a time, challenged the whole Roman Empire.

Fighting a human enemy is one thing … but imagine Hannibal marching into Italy in winter, facing those terrible mountains … facing snow and ice and bitter winds like this, with those poor soldiers and horses and elephants who'd only ever known African sun and warmth ... I'd rather fight ten men single-handed than be out in this ... But Hannibal did it ...

What makes people go on, what makes them not give up?

And yet, before the winter was over, Charles got his troops moving, attacking divisions of the Russian army, scorching the earth after them so that it would be hard for the Russians to follow. But then he was halted by a different kind of weather: a sudden thaw, so that men, horses, waggons and cannons sank into the mud and melted snow.

In any case, Peter was avoiding battle whenever possible. He was well satisfied with his waiting game.

"We can wait as long as Charlie wants," he said, one evening in the inn where his team was staying.

"We can get all the supplies we want from Moscow - food, ammunition, decent uniforms

Southern Russia

The longer we wait, the more Charlie's army turns into a bunch of scarecrows! They've nothing but rags to wear, their boots are falling to pieces, and from what I hear, they've hardly enough dry gun-powder to make it worthwhile carting their cannon along with them. We've got them every which way: they can wait here, getting weaker and weaker, or they can make an attempt on Moscow - but they're far too small and weak a force now for that - or they can go back to their friends in Poland. Whichever way, Moscow's safe. For this year, anyway."

Abraham thought, but didn't say, that from what he'd heard of the Swedish king, he would never go back. He was not the kind to give up. Not when his army had got so far!

What Charles actually did surprised everybody: he didn't go back, and he didn't go forward – instead, he moved his army far down to the south-west, further away from Moscow, but nearer the friendly forces that he was expecting to join him – Muslims from the Tsar's territories, who loathed being ruled by Russians, Muslims from the Sultan's Empire, and also an army from the friendly King of

Abraham Hannibal

Poland. He made his camp near a small town
in the south called Poltava. Few people had
heard of Poltava then; it became a name few
people would forget.

Chapter 21

SPY IN THE SWEDISH CAMP

Poltava was a Russian stronghold – the Russian army had taken it over just the year before. Its city-walls were only earth and wood, but the Russians had put ninety-one cannon around them, and there was a guard of several thousand Russians inside. While Charles was waiting for the friendly forces to arrive, he decided to lay siege to the town, sealing it off from supplies, pounding it with cannon every day - although that used up their precious supplies of gun-powder.

For six weeks, as the weather grew hotter and steamier, the Swedes lay siege to Poltava, blasting it with cannon-balls, digging trenches ever nearer the walls - and dying, as the Russian defenders shot at them from the city walls, as their wounds rotted in the sticky heat, as their food ran out and they had to make do with horse meat and black bread. But the Russians inside Poltava were in trouble too, as *their* supplies of food and ammunition inside the sealed-off town grew lower and lower, and the Swedish trenches came nearer and nearer to the city walls ...

Meanwhile the rest of the Russian army were coming closer - but between them and the town of Poltava lay a wide, marshy river, with steep, high banks, hard to cross at any time, but almost impossible in the teeth of an enemy army. Poltava, and the Swedish camp, were on its west bank; the main Russian army were to the east of the river, a good couple of miles away. Even the Russian cannon were useless: the river was too wide for the cannon-balls to hit the Swedish camp. And Peter was on his way up from checking on his ships, by the Black Sea. His generals waited. They had another reason to wait: over five thousand more troops were expected to join them in a few weeks at the latest.

On June 4th, Peter arrived. Everyone could sense that this time was different: this time wasn't a matter of harassing the edges of each others' armies, or of a few divisions of either army meeting in battle. This time, both armies were assembled, more or less at full strength, each led by its own King, within one small patch of countryside. This time, it was make-or-break.

But still Peter hesitated, sending small groups of men up and down the river, spying and shooting at the far side; he even sent a bigger force right across the river, using the nearest ford, seven miles to the north, but they quickly withdrew when the Swedes fought back strongly. Abraham was nearly beside himself with impatience.

Come ON, Tsar Peter! What are you waiting for THIS time? Let's get in there and at them!

One hot night nearly two weeks after Peter had arrived at Poltava, he was sitting with his generals outside his stuffy little tent.

Although it was late, it was not yet completely dark; even this far south, the summer nights were very short. Abraham sat on the ground with a lamp, slate and chalk, ready to take notes, and bursting to know what decisions would be made.

"If we don't attack, Poltava's going to fall, for sure," said Peter, heavily. "Then it'll become a secure headquarters for the Swedes, which is something we can do without, especially if the Poles and the Turks do send them supporting forces. Poltava would make a very dangerous enemy base indeed. But I'm still not willing to risk my whole army. That river is a terrible barrier to cross; we've tried it already, and had our noses bloodied. My feeling is that we wait till the extra forces arrive - it should only be another week or two."

The generals discussed the matter further, but no-one liked to speak against the Tsar, and the meeting ended.

Abraham was too angry and dissatisfied to sleep; he didn't even undress, but wandered around the camp, his brain whirling with plans and ideas.

Poltava's about to fall; the Swedes are just hungry, ragged scarecrows - the Tsar's said so himself.

Southern Russia

Our army's much bigger than theirs. When ARE we going to get a better chance than this? We're bound to win! There isn't even a risk! Maybe if I could PROVE to the Tsar that the Swedes are in a mess, he'd make up his mind to attack ... But how to do that?

Everywhere men were sitting outside their tents, chatting quietly: it was too hot to sleep, and besides, everyone was on edge: they all knew that after nine years of on-and-off fighting, of a hundred little battles and games of hide-and-seek, the time was coming for The Big One, the battle that would decide everything for Russia, the battle that might see Charles of Sweden marching victorious to Moscow and crowning himself Tsar ... or the battle that would finish him off for good ... and they knew that their army was bigger, healthier, better-fed and much better equipped than Charles's army.

Voices and laughter floated across at Abraham as soldiers spotted him through the summer twilight.

"Look! There's the Tsar's African! Come and join us, African! Come and bring us good luck!"

But Abraham was in no mood for chat. He

made his way through the camp towards the river, and stood on the edge of the low, crumbly bank. There, over on the other side, loomed the walls of Poltava, dark against the last light of the long summer evening, a low mass of houses huddling all around their base.

The Swedes seemed as wakeful as their enemy: here and there a lamp glowed, and there was the faint murmur of thousands of sleepless men keeping busy, moving, talking, mending their kit, grooming their horses ... Somewhere in Poltava, a clock struck eleven, and the clear sound floated across the river ... A bright, almost-full moon had risen.

Suddenly Abraham decided what to do. He darted back to his own tent and changed out of his red and green uniform into plain grey trousers, shirt and sash; he took his cloak, even though it was such a hot night.

Then he went over to where the horses were stabled. As he was with a foot-regiment, and not with the cavalry, he never had the chance to ride into battle - except in his dreams - but he had been an excellent rider as a little boy, and in Russia he'd always grabbed any chance to ride

when he could. He chose a quiet-looking mare, saddled her up, wrapped his cloak round his head and face, and headed north.

I reckon I've got about four hours of near-darkness to get over to their camp and back across the river ... We'll see what we can see ...

Even now that the twilight had faded, the moon was so bright that he could see his way quite clearly - and be seen. He galloped along the top of the steep river-bank, high above the marshy shores and muddy waters; at last he reached the ford, seven miles away, where part of the Russian army had crossed a few days before, but had been pushed back again by the Swedes.

I daren't risk riding across - I'll be seen ... they're bound to have look-outs here. Better tie the mare up in the shadows, and slip across as quietly as I can ...

He took off his breeches, stockings and boots, made them into a bundle inside his cloak, and slipped into the warm, muddy water, holding the bundle over his head. The bottom was soft and slippery, and the water reached his waist, but he crossed without difficulty.

Then he dressed again and, keeping his eyes skinned for guards and look-outs, he began to run south along the other river-bank, far steeper on this side, back down towards Poltava and the Swedish camp. He kept his eyes open for hiding-places, and there were plenty: thick patches of forest, steep gorges in the ground, but until the end he saw no one. It was a long haul, some seven miles, but he was strong and fit, and he kept up a long, fast, steady stride. The problem was where to go, what to do, when he reached the Swedish camp ...

Ahead of him, black against the moonlit

sky, he could see the great mound of the Poltava walls, with here and there a watchman's lamp twinkling, and he thought of his fellow-Russians trapped inside.

Then Abraham came towards the houses of the lower town outside the walls, all taken over as lodgings by the Swedes; beyond, further away from the river, was the main Swedish camp. Here, surely, he would find watchmen …

He waited till his fast-panting breath had quietened down … Slowly, absolutely silently, slipping from shadow to shadow, using trees and bushes as cover, sliding in and out of ditches, he made his way nearer and nearer the town, and at last he slunk into one of its alley-ways, behind the backs of two look-outs who were standing absorbed in a deep discussion.

Somewhere among these houses is the one which King Charles has chosen for himself …

The story had found its way even to the Russian side of the river, of how Charles had deliberately picked a house so close to the fortress that its walls were all pock-marked with bullet-holes and smashed with cannon-balls from the Russian guns on the town walls.

Abraham Hannibal

Abraham placed himself in the shadow of a house-wall and looked at the silvery moonlit scene ahead of him. Although it was the dead of night, he could hear quiet movements and voices everywhere: here too, men found it hard to sleep, for the heat, and for thinking about what the next days would bring ...

He could see the ghostly forms of soldiers, pale in their war-worn uniforms, sitting in the doorways, or wandering up and down the alley-ways, discussing with a kind of urgency in their voices. And although Abraham couldn't pick out a word that was said, he thought he could smell fear in the warm night air, a panic that was barely under control ...

There were guards too, standing at street-corners, on the look-out. He wrapped his cloak round his head and shoulders like a shawl, pulling it over his forehead to throw a deep shadow across his face ... At all costs, no one must see that he was a foreigner ...

Slowly but firmly, so that no one would think him unsure of his way, and keeping in the shadows where he could, Abraham walked up the alley-way towards the town walls, and then, faced with a choice of left or right, turned right along the crooked rows of houses and inns nearest to the fortress - and the Russian guns. The houses were all single storey, their windows and shutters thrown wide open against the stuffy heat; from nearly every house came the glow of lamp or candle light, and the sound of voices. The whole Swedish army seemed awake.

As Abraham crept past, he peered, as discreetly as he could, through every window, searching for any clue. What he did see, again and again, as he glanced quickly in through each window and moved on before he could be spotted, was men in uniforms so faded and patched that he could hardly identify the Swedish colours of blue and yellow, men thin and sick, and, most of all, despairing: whispering anxiously, urgently, among themselves, their pale faces frowning with worry. How different, thought Abraham, from the cheerful soldiers back on his side of the river!

This is an army that's lost its nerve. There's no way THIS army believes it's the finest in all Europe! They've been through too much … Surely we're in with a good chance of beating them now!

And Abraham felt a quick rush of hope inside of him, at the thought of fighting an army that had lost hope ... but he quickly moved on into the next pool of shadows, in case he should be challenged ...

Already he wondered if, over to the east behind the dark mass of the Poltava walls, past the river and his own camp, the sky was beginning to grow lighter ... and one place where he did not want daylight to find him was the enemy camp! A clock struck: once, twice, three times.

Suddenly, Abraham froze. Not far ahead along the alleyway stood two guards - but not on look-out at a street-corner this time: these guards were keeping watch at a doorway, the doorway of a large, solid brick house, though one much blasted by the Russian guns on the town walls. Could this - maybe - be the home of King Charles himself?

Trying not to look shifty, Abraham slipped along the alley to the first window of the house, stood up on tip-toe, and peeped in. And there, by the glow of oil-lamps, he saw the enemy king

at last: not rearing up on a stallion this time, no
slashing and stabbing with his sword, but lying in
his white night-shirt on a blood-stained bed, his
left foot bloody and bandaged, his eyes closed
his face grey and clammy with sweat, his blond
hair matted.

Round the young king stood or sat
Abraham supposed - his generals, their blue-and
yellow uniforms smarter and more splendid than
the common soldiers', their decorations
gleaming, but on their faces exactly the same
expressions of loss and anxiety as Abraham had
seen in the humbler rooms in the town. The
king did not seem to be asleep: he groaned and
tossed, unconscious, in a fever, while the
generals muttered dismally and shook their
heads.

*This is the end for the Swedes! And they know
it! Without him to lead them, they're done for! Peter
MUST make his mind up to go into battle when he
knows this! Pity, though, that I'll never meet Charles
in battle now after all ...*

One of the soldiers on guard duty outside
the king's door suddenly turned and called out
sharply in Abraham's direction. Abraham lifted

Southern Russia

his right hand in a kind of clumsy wave, and turned back as calmly and steadily as he could manage, re-tracing his steps the way he had come. The guard gave another shout; Abraham simply carried on. For a moment, there was stillness behind him, and he thought he was getting away with it.

But then he heard the man's voice calling out again and again, and the thud of boots on the dry earth of the lane. He broke into a run, and darted along the alley-ways, away from the huge pile of the town walls, towards the countryside.

Behind him he could hear not just one man running, but the heavy pounding of many feet; there was the sudden crack of a pistol-shot over his shoulder. His cloak was getting in the way, and he flung it off.

I'll never keep ahead of them ... it's a seven-mile run along the west bank of the river till I get back to the ford ... I'll never keep ahead of them - they're bound to fetch themselves horses ... I could hide in the forest, or in a ditch, but how long for? They'll find me in the end ... And I MUST take Peter this news - while it's still hot, before he hears it from anyone else!

Abraham Hannibal

By now he had got to the edge of the town; ahead of him lay those long miles of countryside before the river-ford where he'd left the mare; behind him he could hear the thud-thud of the Swedish soldiers on his trail.

In a flash, Abraham made up his mind. There was another way: just nearby, to the east of the town walls, was the river - no ford here, as the bank was a steep cliff a good two hundred feet high, but at least it was nearby.

He dashed madly across rough grass and between bushes and trees, doubling up low to try and make himself harder to see. Behind him was still the crashing and thudding of Swedish boots; then there was the crack, once again, of pistol fire, the whistle of a bullet somewhere above his head, and then again and again.

He reached the edge of the cliff, flung himself flat on the grass, and looked at what was below and in front of him. He just had time to take in, two hundred feet below, wide dark patches that he supposed were reeds and rough grass, and then stretches of water or mud that shone greasily in the thin light of dawn, when another bullet whistled over his head.

Clutching hold of two tufts of grass, he swiftly tumbled himself over the edge, and felt for a foothold: the cliff-side was crumbly and soft, with plenty of little ledges and hollows, and here and there bushy plants growing out of it, and he was soon well down below the edge, clambering and sliding as fast as he could, pressing his chest and stomach flat against the soft earth, bits of cliff-side coming away with his hands and feet.

All the time, Abraham was looking down, not up, but he could hear yells above him, and every now and then a clod of earth would fall down from the cliff-edge as the Swedes stamped up and down, or a bullet would whizz down somewhere behind his back towards the marsh below.

He let himself fall the last ten feet or so, squelched on all fours into the muddy edge of the river, and began to wade through the ooze across to the Russian side. Sometimes he stepped up onto the firm foothold of a hard clump of grass, sometimes he sank into the slime up to his thighs, and after he had felt a few bullets fly past not too far away and plop into the water, he was happy to let himself fall headlong into the swamp and carry on half-crawling, half-wallowing, knowing that he was now just a shapeless muddy lump, perfectly camouflaged against the Swedish marksmen on the cliff-top.

Another kind of danger lay ahead, of course: the deeper waters of the real river. Abraham's stomach tightened in panic at the thought of swimming: in all these years, he had never got used to the thought of deep water - too many memories ... In the growing light, he kept his eyes open for something to use as a float, and soon he grabbed at a piece of plank he found stuck in a bush.

At last he felt the water swirling round him faster and deeper, and his feet no longer touched any kind of bottom; his paddling was turning into real swimming. Just managing to keep his panic under control, he splashed his way across the broad stretch of dark, warm water, a powerful current tugging him over and down-stream, until he reached the marshy eastern shore.

Soon Abraham was scrambling up the

river-bank - much lower, fortunately, than the one on the western side - and dripped and squished his way into the Russian camp, just as a bright, clear dawn was breaking behind it. A cock crowed, and he felt like shouting out aloud himself.

He found Peter sitting on a camp-stool outside his tent, shaving, a page-boy holding a basin of foamy water under his chin. The Tsar stared at him.

"GOOD HEAVENS, lad! What pond have YOU been sleeping in?"

"I've come from the Swedish side of the river ... Your Majesty," panted Abraham. "I've got news ... good news ... important news."

Peter handed his razor to the page-boy.

"YES! YES! Spit it out! Spit it out!"

"King Charles is desperately ill. He's been shot in the foot, he's got a fever. There's no way he could lead his army. The Swedes' nerve has completely gone - they look completely lost without him."

"WELL! We'll hear the whole story later, of how the devil you found out! We move the entire army across, starting today! The time has ruly come for our armies to meet! You will be rewarded, boy, you will be rewarded, never fear!"

And he gave Abraham a clap across his nuddy shoulders that nearly knocked him lying.

Chapter 22

FOR THE GLORY OF RUSSIA

Over the next four days, the whole huge body of the Russian army, all forty-two thousand men of it, was jumping with activity. The tents were struck, the waggons were loaded, and at last the cavalry and then the foot soldiers made their way slowly up the east bank of the river to the ford seven miles north where Abraham had left his mare and waded across that fateful day when some Russian sharp shooter had shot across the river and by chance wounded a king. (No one ever found out for certain who had done it, though a good few people claimed to have been responsible!)

For two whole days, the river was full of lines of men and horses, cannons and waggons crossing over from the east to the west bank, and at last the two armies were on the same side of the river. This time, they met no resistance.

Slowly the Russians began to work their way down towards the Swedes. Peter's plan was to build a strong camp or fort about half-way between the ford and Poltava: a square of huge earth walls, with a deep ditch at the front, open at the back where the steep river-bank plunged down behind, so that no enemy army could possibly attack. Overnight the soldiers worked, and by morning, the fort walls were up.

Just as in Saint Petersburg or Moscow, Peter wasn't just barking out commands, but sweated away with the men, leaping from one job to another, digging and heaving the earth himself, stamping and smoothing it down, helping to drag the heavy cannons up onto the walls - with Abraham energetically making sure that *he* wasn't left behind.

No one's going to say I'm slacker than my Tsar!

Meanwhile, Charles lay close to death - but, in the end, like the tough fighter that he was, he pulled through. There was no chance, however, of him riding into battle or leading his own troops. As the Russian army was moving across the river, his mood, and the mood of his soldiers, grew gloomier and gloomier. Food supplies were low, and they were short of cannons, bullets and dry gunpowder.

On a steamy Saturday afternoon, as the midday heat was just beginning to wear off, nine days after Abraham's night-time visit to Poltava, Peter inspected his troops.

Thirty-two thousand foot-soldiers had their tents pitched inside the earth fort, ten thousand horsemen were positioned on the rough plains outside.

"Get me the troops drawn up in parade formation," barked Peter to his generals. "Let's see what they look like. And I'd like to speak to as many as can hear me at one time."

Regiment after regiment of infantry lined up inside the fort, in their uniforms of bright red and green, in their shining high black boots and three-cornered hats, row upon row of muskets with sharp bayonets gleaming, propped on shoulders in perfectly matching diagonals.

Southern Russia

Flags waved only limply in the heavy, dead air, but the bugles and flutes and drums made up for that with a fine din: everyone was in high spirits, and the musicians had the best chance to show it.

Abraham was beside himself with pride and excitement as, along with the other drummer-boys, he rat-tat-tatted his regiment into formation. The cavalry lined up on the outside of the fort, their steel breastplates and backplates, their drawn swords, all glinting in the evening sunlight, the horses whinnying and fidgeting, as if they too knew that a great day was coming.

Peter was mounted on his favourite brown stallion, and slowly rode up and down the lines of infantry, then went out through the heavy rough door and inspected his cavalry, nodding with satisfaction. At last he returned, dismounted, climbed up onto the south-west corner of the fort wall, and looked out over the thousands of his soldiers. Abraham, as one of the drummers of Peter's own star regiment, was standing just below, and could almost meet his eyes.

Abraham Hannibal

There was absolute silence, broken only by the occasional snickering or stamping of an over-frisky horse on the plains outside. Abraham saw Peter lick his dry lips, and heard him clear his throat. The Tsar raised his voice as loud as he could.

"Soldiers: the hour has struck when the fate of the whole motherland lies in your hands. Either it will be the end of Russia, or she will be re-born a finer and stronger country. Do not think you are fighting for Peter: you are fighting for the survival and the glory of Russia!"

There was a tiny pause; then a great roar broke out from thousands of throats, swelling back, wave after wave, across the ranks, as the men further back, who hadn't heard a word, picked up the cheer from the soldiers in front. On and on it went, as the foot-soldiers waved their hats above their heads, and the horsemen brandished their swords or fired pistols up into the air:

"THE GLORY OF RUSSIA! THE GLORY OF RUSSIA! THE GLORY OF RUSSIA!"

And, with a sudden great lurch of excitement in his stomach, Abraham thought,

Southern Russia

At last! This really is going to be it. And I did my part, getting us all moving across the river when we did. It was me who pushed this battle into happening!

Chapter 23

THE GREAT BATTLE

In fact, Peter, cautious as ever, waited for the Swedes to make the first move, and the whole of the next day was taken up with waiting, and building extra earth-and-wood barriers in the plain between Poltava and the Russian fort, each barrier lined with plenty of cannons, to hold up the Swedish advance.

Then, that night, or rather, very early the following morning, in the first light of dawn, as the foot-soldiers inside the fort were just finishing dressing and arming, Abraham heard it start: down towards Poltava, the roar of the Russian cannons at the barriers they'd built, the crash of musket fire, a confused din of clashing swords, yells, drums and bugle-blasts.

Southern Russia

Abraham grabbed some bread and scrambled up onto the wall of the fort to see what was going on. It was hard to make sense of: about half a mile away to the south-west, across the track to Poltava, he could just see a blur of dust and smoke billowing up against the faint dawn light.

As daylight grew, Abraham could begin to make out in the distance, the faint blue-and-yellow smudge of the Swedish army clashing and merging with the Russian red-and-green. Peter climbed up onto the wall to watch too, but still he did not call out the troops inside the fort. Soldiers climbed up to man all the cannon on the fort walls, but the rest waited by their tents.

The roar and smoke of battle still came from the Russian barriers as the Swedes tried to get across and between them, against the terrible force of the Russian cannons. The watchers on the walls of the fort could just make out the waves of Swedish infantry and cavalry breaking on the barriers, men and horses dropping in their hundreds, and then in their thousands.

Then at last, the watchers saw dribs and drabs of the Swedish army slowly beginning to break through and past the Russian barriers, and re-position themselves on the plain in front of the fort; others escaped sideways into the woods.

Two more hours went by; the morning sun grew high and scorching hot, and at last came the words that Abraham had been waiting for.

"All troops inside this fort to prepare for battle. We are to advance out into open ground!"

Swiftly and smoothly, the Russian infantry began to pour out from the fort entrances, across the rough bridges over the deep ditch they had dug in the days before, and spread themselves out in front of the fort in a long, thick curve, their cavalry arranged at either end.

Over the Russian soldiers' heads, up on the fort walls, were dozens of Russian cannons, pointing out towards the enemy, with dozens more cannons down on the plain, placed right at the front of the Russian lines. Facing them were the pitifully small forces of the Swedes, with no cannons at all.

Peter rode up and down the lines on his

favourite Arab stallion. He pulled his sword from its sheath, held it high, and cried,

"THE GLORY OF RUSSIA! THE GLORY OF RUSSIA! THE GLORY OF RUSSIA!"

And once again the cry swelled through the Russian ranks.

"THE GLORY OF RUSSIA! THE GLORY OF RUSSIA! THE GLORY OF RUSSIA!"

And Abraham joined his voice to the roar of all those tens of thousands of Russian voices.

This is what I've been waiting for! It's happening to me at last! This is what Father expected of me!

As the cry faded, another sound began to be heard: the thin rat-tat-tat of drums, as what was left of the Swedish infantry began to march across the plain, their blue-and-yellow banners bravely flying ... began to march towards the whole huge Russian army, a force five time as big ...

Abraham stared in wonderment. Cannon-balls whistled from the cannons on top of the Russian fort and the cannons at the front of the Russian lines, chopping bloody holes in the Swedish ranks, and still the soldiers came, never firing a shot, their lines never wavering. Closer and closer came the Swedes, across the rough open plain, until Abraham was told to rat-tat-tat the command to kneel and fire muskets.

The Russian bullets ploughed into those thin bodies, splattering their faded blue-and-yellow uniforms with red, and still the Swedish lines never faltered.

Now I see why Tsar Peter's always been so nervous of the Swedish army. It's not just Charles who doesn't know fear! These must be the best soldiers in the world! They haven't got a chance, not a chance! But you'd never know, to look at them!

And, for a second, a cold shiver of pity took hold of him, pity at the hopeless bravery of Charles's men, pity at the pain and the waste of it … but then, all at once, there was no time for pity, as suddenly the Swedes were on them, still without firing, but stabbing and slashing with their sharp bayonets, driving the Russians backwards, shouting some strange war-cry.

And then Abraham began to hear the crack of musket-fire, not just from his own army, behind and alongside him, but also from the Swedes ahead.

They're firing … they're finally firing at us!

Southern Russia

Where's Tsar Peter? WHERE IS HE? Riding through the infantry right in the line of fire, towering over everybody on that huge great stallion of his – nobody could miss him! WHERE IS HE?

Abraham saw the Tsar at last, over to his left, quite far away, slashing down at the Swedes with his sword, a fine sight as his stallion reared above the troops, wheeling to left and right. All seemed well so far, and as the battle roared, Abraham looked for the Tsar's towering figure whenever he could.

Just checking, Your Majesty! Watch out, for God's sake! You're a perfect sitting target!

But one time, as Abraham found himself near Peter, and his eyes anxiously followed him across the confusion of swords and guns, smoke and dust and blood, he heard through the din of cannon and screaming and musket-shots, the crack of one shot and the whistle as the bullet flew toward the Tsar. He saw Peter jerk backwards, gasp fiercely, and clutch his chest.

Abraham's heart went cold as he scrambled near to his Tsar.

"Are you hurt, sir? Are you hurt?"

The Tsar was looking down at his chest

with a strange expression on his face; he brought his hand away, and it was black, not red.

"My uniform is severely wounded, my boy - torn and burnt. But praise be the Mother of God, the bullet seems to have bounced off my holy medal. I am fit and well!"

Abraham gasped. "But you must watch out, sir," he shouted. "It would take a blind Swede to miss you, high above your infantry like this!"

But the Tsar only grinned, and shouted down at him,

"I know - I've had a shot through my saddle already, and one through my hat! Today is not my dying day, that's clear enough!"

And Peter wheeled round his horse, and hacked with his sword at a Swedish soldier who was aiming a pistol at him.

Over to Abraham's right, some Swedes were clambering over Russian bodies towards one of the cannons, and slashing with their swords at the Russian gunners who were firing it. Suddenly Abraham guessed what they were planning to do - and he was right. The Swedes heaved the cannon round so that it was facing *away* from their forces, and back *towards* the Russians and their camp.

Abraham could see that other Swedish soldiers had the same idea - but what to do about it? He couldn't fight with just a pair of drumsticks. He looked down, and saw lying at his feet a Russian soldier, a great bloody wound in his chest, his musket tumbled at his side. Abraham grabbed at it and scrambled over to the nearest cannon. Five Swedes were in the middle of hacking down the Russian gunners who were trying to defend it. One Swede had his back to him, and hardly knowing what he was doing, Abraham shouted out,

"HEY, YOU! SWEDE!"

With one hand, Abraham grabbed the Swede by the shoulder of his uniform and pulled him round to face him. He was a boy, a fair-haired boy hardly older than Abraham, and his blue eyes were wide with surprise.

Abraham held his musket round the middle – and stabbed the Swedish boy hard in the stomach with the bayonet. That instant, he saw another of the Swedes leaping towards him with his sword raised. He tugged the bayonet out

again, and swept the musket round so as to fetch the Swede a great crack across the chin that knocked him out cold.

The fair-haired boy lay in a puddle of blood at Abraham's feet. For an instant, the battle seemed to freeze around him, the din and turmoil to grow still. His head swam dizzily.

I've killed my first enemy. I've killed an enemy … This is what real soldiers do … nothing's ever going to be the same again …

But then came a cheerful shout of "Well done, the Tsar's African!" from an old Russian gunner, as he shot another Swede in the shoulder with his musket, leaving him to crumple groaning on the ground, and Abraham quickly pulled himself together. There seemed to be only three Russians left to fire the cannon.

"D'you need me to help you man this gun?" he asked.

"And welcome!" shouted the old gunner.

So Abraham stood in the thick of the fighting, as the Swedish infantry surged forward, and the first Russian line fell back under the shock of their attack. For something like twenty minutes, he left the drumming to the other drummer-boys, and he and the three gunners kept the cannon firing, and fought off any Swedes who tried to capture it.

But then, little-by-little, they began to notice a change in the pace of the battle: the Swedes had broken the middle of the Russian line, but their numbers were not big enough to keep the attack going, and little-by-little their strength was fading, they were simply being swallowed up by the huge numbers of Russians around them.

And, while Abraham, Tsar Peter, and every single Russian soldier knew that the Swedes always followed their infantry attacks with a terrifying, unbeatable cavalry charge, this time it simply didn't come. The old gunner guessed the reason.

"Hear that cannon-fire just north of us? Reckon the Swedish cavalry are getting pretty heavy punishment - there's nothing they can do against the guns up on the fort walls. They're just being cut to ribbons. This is rough ground for cavalry, anyway - too many ravines and trees in the way!"

"I wish I could see Charles."

Abraham Hannibal

"Leading his army flat on his back on a stretcher? Is it any wonder they're having trouble?"

Peter, on the other hand, was continually where he could see his troops and they could see him - up on his brown stallion, now with the infantry, now with the cavalry, directing and cheering them on.

Chapter 24

VICTORY!

And so, as the sun blazed down from high in the hazy blue sky, some eight hours after the battle had started in the first light of dawn, the Swedish drummers beat the signal to retreat; the Swedish army and the Swedish King retreated back to their camp, leaving only their dead, their wounded, and their prisoners on the battlefield of Poltava; little-by-little the echo of the last shots and the sharp smell of gun-powder faded from the hot air, and the swirls of dust and smoke settled.

Peter waved his hat in the air - the hat with a Swedish bullet-hole in it - and called out from his stallion,

"All-merciful God has granted us victory! The enemy army has been well and truly knocked on the head! Let all able-bodied troops come together to give thanks to God!"

And as the dead and wounded were carried into the fort, thousands of Russians troops gathered in front of it, filthy from gun-smoke and blood and dust, the cavalry-men standing by their heads of their panting and exhausted horses, holding their bridles, soothing them, and a priest led the army in prayers. Then Peter announced,

"All men at ease! Back to camp and dinner!"

And the troops all gave a great cheer.

But there was one person who not ready to leave the battlefield of Poltava till he had got some answers. Abraham had kept near Peter's side since the end of the battle, waiting to speak to him. The Tsar was just about to mount his stallion and ride with his generals into the fort, and Abraham was thinking fast about how to attract his attention, when Peter suddenly noticed him.

"Ah-ha! My young African! I've seen fine work from you these last days!"

"That's what I would like to speak to you

about! Your Majesty, have I shown myself worthy of your trust?"

"Abraham, Russia owes you a debt. You provided most valuable news from the Swedish camp, at a considerable risk to yourself. That was a brave and well-planned act, and I promised you it would be rewarded!"

"And in the battle?"

The Tsar looked down at him, a strange half-smile on his face.

"I think I noticed Gunner Abraham defending a cannon against Swedish attack, and then manning it in fine style! I have a feeling that your days as a drummer-boy are over, and your days as my servant too, for that matter!"

Abraham's eyes widened.

I'm no longer a servant! I'm no longer a servant!

Suddenly he was conscious of all the Princes and Generals standing around him and the Tsar, watching and waiting silently. The thousands of troops behind them were not silent or still, but they were waiting too, waiting for the Tsar to enter the fort before they did.

Abraham tried to clear his throat: it was very dry.

"It would be one of my dearest wishes to serve Your Majesty as an officer of the Russian army."

The Tsar laughed.

"Fine. And what might your other dearest wishes be?"

"Your Majesty, long ago, I left my country on a mission to the Sun King. I still hope to fulfil my mission, to visit the Sun King's court and deliver greetings from the Emperor of Ethiopia."

"Well, I think that wouldn't be too hard to arrange. Let's see ... your officer training can begin here, and at a suitable time we can send you to France for further studies. You have a gift for building and engineering, and the French lead the field in the building of fortresses. I feel that if you specialise in that, you'll be bringing a valuable skill to Russia. And while you're in France, by all means let's have you presented to the French court!"

The Tsar put his huge hand on Abraham's shoulder.

"You know, Abraham, that was one of my better ideas, I feel, removing you from the Sultan's Palace. African or not, you are a better

Russian than many a Russian I've known. Thank you for what you have done for our country. I'd like to see you go far, here in our new Russia. After all, we've had plenty of Scottish and German Generals in our army ... why shouldn't the Tsar's African make it to General one day - eh, Abraham?"

Abraham felt his cheeks go hot, but he nodded as calmly as he could. And then, as the Tsar swung himself up on his horse and rode off with his Generals towards dinner in the fort, Abraham looked around at the battlefield of Poltava, still choked with soldiers and horses, bodies living and dead, and scattered with a mess of abandoned cannon, banners, swords and muskets; he looked around at the earth, the grass and the bushes soaked with blood and smudged with soot.

Somewhere off to the south, what was left of the Swedish army was frantically getting ready to escape south towards the Empire of the Sultan. Abraham felt almost suffocated by the strength of his feelings.

Well, the battle of Poltava's over. Sweden really has been knocked on the head for a long, long time.

Abraham Hannibal

We've won, and I've won. It's a new beginning for Russia and for Tsar Peter! And a new beginning for me!

Lahia, you always said, if you want something badly enough, and don't give up wanting it, you'll get it in the end. Soon I'll be in France, and at last the Sun King will see what us Ethiopians are made of!

As the lines of troops piled in through the gates of the fort for their dinner, Abraham stood very still, looking out over the blood and filth and mess of the battlefield, and whispered under his breath the French words he had learnt so long ago.

"My name is Abraham, and my father is a noble lord of Africa. The Emperor of Ethiopia sends brotherly greetings to the King of the Franks."

AFTERWORD

Abraham was a real person. He himself wrote how his father was an African Prince, and how he was taken from his home to Istanbul when he was a little boy, and then to Russia. His family used to describe him weeping, as an old man, when he remembered his favourite sister drowning in the sea as his ship sailed away from the coast of Africa.

Some of the details of this story are made up, but many of the characters really existed: the Emperor Jesus the Great of Ethiopia, Doctor Poncet, the King of Mecca and his raiders (who really did kidnap the Ethiopian children on their way to France), King Louis XIV of France, Peter Tolstoy, Fatty Savva, King Charles XII of Sweden, and, of course, all the Russian royal family. Elizabeth is based on a real person too, a French girl called Aimee.

Another real person was the famous African general Hannibal who is buried near

Istanbul: Abraham took his name as a surname when he was older.

Abraham really did get to France in the end, and met the Sun King's great-grandson, Louis XV, but he didn't spend his life there. He became an officer in Tsar Peter's favourite regiment, and worked mostly as an engineer, designing fortresses and canals. He also tutored the next Tsar, the young son of Prince Alexis, in Maths.

Tsar Peter managed to start turning Russia into a strong and modern country, and St Petersburg, "Peter's city", really did grow out of a swamp to become one of the loveliest cities in the world.

When Peter and then Catherine died, Abraham lost his two most powerful friends, and he spent three terrible years exiled in Siberia. After that, life began to improve, and he became a General in the army, governing the Russian troops in the port-city today called Tallinn. He also became a very rich land-owner.

Abraham got married twice, and had a large family; one of his sons, Ivan, became a famous General and Admiral. Another of his sons, Osip, had a daughter, Nadezhda, who married a nobleman called Sergei Pushkin ... and they had a son called Alexander Pushkin, who became one of the most famous writers in Russia ... and wrote a story about his great-grandfather called ...

THE AFRICAN OF PETER THE GREAT

The Ethiopian Alphabet

On the opposite page you can see the alphabet
that Abraham, like other Ethiopian children, had
to learn - except that the full Ethiopian alphabet
has even more letters - lots more!

Actually, the signs don't stand for single letters - they
stand for whole syllables. For example, the sign for
'ha' (as in 'hat') is ሀ, and there are different tiny changes
to this sign for the other vowel sounds, like this:
ሀ ha   ሁ hoo   ሂ hee   ሃ haa   ሄ hey   ህ hi   ሆ ho
(as in hat)(as in hoot)(as in heat)(as in hard)(as in hey!)(as in his)(as in horse)

So, for example, the name of Abraham's sister Lahia
would look like this: ላሒያ   ላ laa   ሒ hee   ያ ya
Can you find all the signs on the chart opposite?

The name of his father Fares would look like this:
ፈሬስ   ፈ fa   ሬ rey   ስ s (the little vowel after the
's' isn't pronounced) Can you find these signs too?

PUZZLE

See if you can use the chart opposite to read the words
in the picture of Abraham writing on the floor of the
ship's hold in Chapter 4.   The answers are at the
end of the AUTHOR'S THANK YOU pages.

Try writing your names or your friends' names
the Ethiopian way - or use the alphabet as your
code for writing top-secret messages!

ሀ ha	ሁ hoo	ሂ hee	ሃ haa	ሄ hey	ህ hi	ሆ ho
ለ la	ሉ loo	ሊ lee	ላ laa	ሌ ley	ል li	ሎ lo
መ ma	ሙ moo	ሚ mee	ማ maa	ሜ mey	ም mi	ሞ mo
ሰ sa	ሱ soo	ሲ see	ሳ saa	ሴ sey	ስ si	ሶ so
ረ ra	ሩ roo	ሪ ree	ራ raa	ሬ rey	ር ri	ሮ ro
ሸ sha	ሹ shoo	ሺ shee	ሻ shaa	ሼ shey	ሽ shi	ሾ sho
በ ba	ቡ boo	ቢ bee	ባ baa	ቤ bey	ብ bi	ቦ bo
ጠ ta	ጡ too	ጢ tee	ጣ taa	ጤ tey	ጥ ti	ጦ to
ነ na	ኑ noo	ኒ nee	ና naa	ኔ ney	ን ni	ኖ no
አ a	ኡ oo	ኢ ee	ኣ aa	ኤ ey	እ i	ኦ o
ከ ka	ኩ koo	ኪ kee	ካ kaa	ኬ key	ክ ki	ኮ ko
ወ wa	ዉ woo	ዊ wee	ዋ waa	ዌ wey	ው wi	ዎ wo
ዘ za	ዙ zoo	ዚ zee	ዛ zaa	ዜ zey	ዝ zi	ዞ zo
የ ya	ዩ yoo	ዪ yee	ያ yaa	ዬ yey	ይ yi	ዮ yo
ደ da	ዱ doo	ዲ dee	ዳ daa	ዴ dey	ድ di	ዶ do
ጀ ja	ጁ joo	ጂ jee	ጃ jaa	ጄ jey	ጅ ji	ጆ jo
ገ ga	ጉ goo	ጊ gee	ጋ gaa	ጌ gey	ግ gi	ጎ go
ፈ fa	ፉ foo	ፊ fee	ፋ faa	ፌ fey	ፍ fi	ፎ fo
ፐ pa	ፑ poo	ፒ pee	ፓ paa	ፔ pey	ፕ pi	ፖ po

THE RUSSIAN ALPHABET

Once Abraham got to Moscow, Tsar Peter soon had him learning to read and write in Russian. You can see most of the Russian alphabet on the opposite page. It works more or less like the English alphabet, except that it has 33 letters or special signs instead of 26.

This is what Abraham's full name that he used when he was older, looks like in Russian:

Аврам	Петрович	Ганнибал
Avram	Petrovich	Gannibal

You can see that 'Abraham' in Russian is pronounced a bit differently from the English way. Abraham took his middle name 'Petrovich' which means 'son of Peter', because Peter was his godfather. (All Russians have to use a middle name like this which means 'son/daughter of so-and-so'). Finally, he took 'Hannibal' as a surname, after the famous African general, but as Russian doesn't have an H, it is spelled with a G at the beginning.

PUZZLE

See if you can use the chart opposite to find out the Russian names for the animals that Abraham drew for little Prince Peter in Chapter 11.

Can you figure out which Russian cities these are?

Москва   Санкт Петербург

The answers are at the end of the AUTHOR'S THANK YOU pages. Try writing your name or your friends' names the Russian way - or use the alphabet as your code for writing top-secret messages!

$\mathcal{A}$ a	a as in <u>a</u>rt	Π n	p as in <u>p</u>ot
$\mathcal{B}$ δ	b as in <u>b</u>ox	$\mathcal{P}$ p	r as in <u>r</u>at
$\mathcal{B}$ δ	v as in <u>v</u>isit	C c	s as in <u>s</u>it
$\mathcal{T}$ z	g as in <u>g</u>ate	$\mathcal{T}$ $\bar{m}$ т	t as in <u>t</u>op
$\mathcal{D}$ g ∂	d as in <u>d</u>uck	$\mathcal{Y}$ y	oo as in sh<u>oo</u>t
$\mathcal{E}$ e	ye as in <u>ye</u>t	$\mathcal{F}$ φ	f as in <u>f</u>ox
$\ddot{\mathcal{E}}$ $\ddot{e}$	yo as in <u>yo</u>nder	$\mathcal{X}$ x	ch as in lo<u>ch</u>
$\mathcal{K}$ $\mathcal{H}$	s as in mea<u>s</u>ure	$\mathcal{U}$ $\mathcal{u}$	ts as in <u>T</u>sar
$\mathcal{3}$ z z	z as in <u>z</u>oo	$\mathcal{Y}$ $\mathcal{r}$	ch as in <u>ch</u>ick
$\mathcal{U}$ u	ee as in f<u>ee</u>t	$\mathcal{U}$ $\mathcal{u}$	sh as in <u>sh</u>op
$\breve{\mathcal{U}}$ $\breve{u}$	y as in bo<u>y</u>	$\mathcal{U}$ $\mathcal{u}$	<u>sh</u> <u>ch</u> - po<u>sh</u> <u>ch</u>ina
$\mathcal{K}$ κ	k as in <u>k</u>ing	ы	y as in ph<u>y</u>sics
$\mathcal{A}$ $\mathcal{n}$	l as in <u>l</u>ion	$\mathcal{J}$ $\mathcal{э}$	e as in l<u>e</u>t
$\mathcal{M}$ $\mathcal{u}$	m as in <u>m</u>at	$\mathcal{HO}$ $\mathcal{ю}$	yu as in <u>yu</u>le
$\mathcal{H}$ $\mathcal{н}$	n as in <u>n</u>ut	$\mathcal{Я}$ $\mathcal{я}$	ya as in <u>ya</u>rd
O o	o as in b<u>o</u>re		

AUTHOR'S THANK YOU

I would like to thank everybody who helped to make this book happen. They are too many for me to mention them all, but here are some of them:

Stephen (Huey) Bell, for helping to look after our son, Abraham, while I was getting this book ready

Eric Robson, my wonderful artist

Rita and Professor Richard Pankhurst, Assefa Gabre Mariam, Gabre Medhin and his family, Ato Mitiku and Ato Aforki, who helped me in Ethiopia or Eritrea

John and Berrin Scott, Andrew and Caroline Finkel, and Professor Jamal Kafadar, who helped me in Istanbul

Vera and Professor Leonid Arenshtein, Irina and Nina Yureva, Professor Tony Briggs, Natasha Olshanskaya, Professor Mark

Sokolyansky, Boris Kurashov, Gennadi and
Valentina Kokin, Vitaly and Nadia Andreev,
Dr David Parrott, Dr Tim Binyon, and Tatiana
Wolf, who helped me in the Ukraine, Russia
or England

Umberto Allemandi, John Aldridge, Keith
Gaines, Perilla Kinchin, Alastair Sawday
and Lucy Bramley, who all helped me
with the publishing side of things

the adults and children who read and
commented on the manuscript – Marilyn
Malin, Chris McDonagh, Anna Somers Cocks,
Peggy Somers Cocks, Susan Powell, Charlotte
Rolfe, Andrew Thomas, Shomari Charles,
Patrick Schrijnen, Martha Paren,
Katherine Hardy

Answers to Russian Alphabet Puzzles

Sankt Peterburg – Saint Petersburg

Moskva – Moscow   slon – elephant

zebra – zebra   lev – lion   zhiraf – giraffe

Answers to Ethiopian Alphabet Puzzle

(bottom row) Andrew

(middle row) Elizabeth   Nagonga

(top row) Abraham

SHORT BIBLIOGRAPHY

I researched Abraham's story and the background information as carefully and widely as I could. Here are some of the sources I used:

Lesley BLANCH: *The Wilder Shores of Love* (London, 1954)

Fernand BRAUDEL: *The Mediterranean and the Mediterranean World in the Age of Philip II* (English edition, London, 1972)

Angus KONSTAM: *Poltava 1709 – Russia Comes of Age* (London, 1994)

Georg LEETS: *Abraham Petrovich Hannibal, a biography* (published in Russian, Tallin, 1984)

Bernard LEWIS: *Race and Slavery in the Middle East* (New York, 1990)

Raphaela LEWIS: *Everyday Life in Ottoman Turkey* (London, 1971)

Robert K MASSIE: *Peter the Great – his Life and World* (UK edition, London, 1981)

Vladimir NABOKOV: introduction to his translation of *Eugene Onegin*, by Alexander Pushkin (London, 1964)

Richard PANKHURST: *An Introduction to the Economic History of Ethiopia from Early times to 1800* (London, 1961)

N.M. PENZER: *The Harem* (London, 1936)

Charles PONCET: *A Voyage to Aethiopia* Joseph PITTS: *A Faithful Account of the Religion and Manners of the Mahometans*; both reprinted by the Hakluyt Society (1949) under the title *The Red Sea and Adjacent Countries at the Close of the Seventeenth Century*

NOTE ON ABRAHAM'S COUNTRY OF BIRTH

All through this book, and the one before it, **ABRAHAM HANNIBAL and the Raiders of the Sands**, Abraham's homeland is referred to as Ethiopia. In fact, nowadays, much of the north-eastern part of Abraham's Ethiopia is a separate country called Eritrea. I have used the name Ethiopia in these books as it was the name used in Abraham's time for all the lands ruled by his Emperor, including the lands ruled under him by the Lord of the Sea.

NOTE ON UKRAINE AND RUSSIA

Several parts of this story take place in the country known as Ukraine, to the south of Russia. In Tsar Peter's day, much of Ukraine was under Russian rule, and to simplify the geography of the story, it is referred to in this book as Southern Russia.

Read about Abraham's adventures in Ethiopia and Arabia in

ABRAHAM HANNIBAL

and the Raiders of the Sands

Meet Abraham's sister, Lahia, and his pet lion, Nimrod. Find out how his father captured his mother – and then married her. Brave the crocodiles of the Terrible River with him, and pick your way along steep and slippery mountain paths. Find out about the mysterious obelisks and magnificent Palaces of Abraham's homeland. Meet Abraham's Emperor, Jesus the Great, and learn why he sent a young boy on a mission to another world …

Who *are* the fearsome Raiders of the Sands, and how does Abraham escape their clutches?

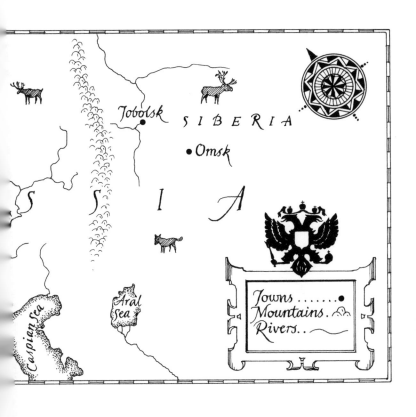

Tobolsk

S I B E R I A

•Omsk

S   S   I   A

Caspian Sea

Aral Sea

Towns . . . . •
Mountains . . .⌢⌢
Rivers . .〰

Map of
ABRAHAM HANNIBAL'S
Journey to Russia

Abraham's journey ------
Towns .... ●
Mountains .... ⌒⌒
Rivers ....